I Ar

Dear Loraine

coda.

The Submission Series - nine

Thank You for Coming

CD Reiss

CD Reiss

DEDICATION

My dear son, if you are reading this, I hope I am dead. But if I'm not, put it down. I'm your mother. This is totally inappropriate reading material.

This book hasn't been edited. I cranked out a print edition for a signing. If you want something with better editing, don't buy this one.

And I know the formatting is screwy in places. I'm sorry. This is not the edition for perfectionists.

CHAPTER 1.

JONATHAN

I brushed my thumb against her nipple, bending it, then I leaned down to suck it. She wove her fingers in my hair. I tasted the water of the shower on her, the tinge of soap on my tongue. Steam still fogged the room.

"Jonathan," she whispered. "I'll miss the plane."

"No you won't."

I drew my tongue down her belly, flat and tight, stopping at the navel bar she still wore for me, then down between her legs. I bent one of her knees and put it over my shoulder, giving my mouth access to her.

"I haven't packed yet," she said, but I knew I had her. I opened her lips with my thumbs and licked her clit slowly, tip to taint and back again, tasting the fresh, clean skin and clear, rushing fluids.

"Pack fast," I said. She'd be gone for a week. I wanted her before she left.

"I have to pack the Theremin and it's oh, God," she moaned when I sucked her, hitching her other leg over my shoulder. "Delicate. Jesus, what is with you lately?"

I stood up and wiped my mouth with my hand. She sat spread eagled on the bathroom vanity, wet and ready. She was mine, and I loved her.

"What's with me lately?" I was in my underwear, which I didn't bother taking off as I pulled my dick out. "Maybe I'm bored."

"You could work again."

"I could."

I slid in nice and easy.

There was a feeling, as I fucked her on the vanity, that something wasn't quite right. Something

3

was missing. She was wet. I was hard. Her tits bounced when I thrust and there was enough nudity between us to get my dick inside her.

But her arms. I didn't know where they were going next. She moved in unexpected ways. I put my arms around her, holding her together and I leaned in close to kiss her, dragging my stubble on her cheek and the sensitive part of her neck. She whispered, *ouch*.

I felt suddenly powerful. I'd been fucking her for months with this borrowed thing in my chest, but when she said ouch, I wanted to more than fuck her. I wanted to tear her apart.

I lost my shit at the thought of it, coming in her the way I'd been since the hospital, without control or intent; just because I was ready.

Monica came a second after I started, and we gripped each other, quivering. The steam had barely cleared the mirrors when I kissed her shoulder and realized I had a problem in my arms.

***

I stretched out in the sun with my scarred chest to the sky and felt that thing beating. The July heat baked me, muggy and sticky, sharing sweat with a stranger's tissue, grateful to be alive, yet in a state of constant bewilderment, thinking, how the fuck was I pulled from death for this? And who was I? I'd eaten and enjoyed blowtorch-spicy food, and suddenly, I found it intolerable. And I felt a pull to run that I knew, intuitively came from the same place. I jogged in the morning, and if Monica was away I jogged at night. I loved it. The burn in my throat the fully energized exhaustion when I'd pushed myself too hard and too long. But I'd never wanted to run before. The desire wasn't mine, it belonged to the heart, which had grown in someone else. Was I till wholly me? I pondered it too often, and for too long.

"Hey," Monica said, stepping into my sunlight. She wore a pale blue dress and clunky bracelets. "I'm going."

I patted a place for her to sit next to me.

"I can't," she said. "Lil's waiting."

I flipped my sunglasses up so I could look her in the eye and with that gaze, let her know I was entitled to a minute of her time.

"Goddess."

"I'll call you when I land." She bent to kiss me, and when her lips hit mine I held her head there an extra few seconds. She smiled and trotted away.

I had a problem. She was going to Caracas for three days to open two shows with some madhouse band, and I wasn't going with her by doctor's orders. Not yet.

The impulsive side of me wanted to follow her, and let the team of highly-paid specialists kiss my ass, but I stayed behind. There was no need to rush. Three more days wouldn't change anything.

When I'd met Monica, I'd known what I was. Who I was. I knew what I was made of and I knew how to get what I wanted. I'd still been in love with my idea of my ex wife, but my goddess had cured me of that.

I thought being happy was what had made me demand control in the bedroom, but I was wrong, or at least only partly right. All the soul-searching in the world had led me to a false conclusion.

I'd been dominant because I knew myself, and in knowing myself, I had the confidence to bind and hit and hurt, because I'd know when to stop.

5

We got home from the hospital, Monica and I, and eventually made love again. Still, I wasn't myself. I was mostly me and partly someone else. An alien piece of meat had been lodged in me. I didn't know what it would do. Would it beat right for me, or for the person it was meant for? Would it skip a beat at the sight of some strange woman? Would it break over a different past or a lost present? I kept imagining it jumped out of me like a frog on a frying pan, slapping to the kitchen floor with a *splat*, beating on the tiles, squirting yellow plasma. Once, I dreamed it bounced out of me and landed in the pool, swimming with Sheila in a trail of curly red blood. And I laughed, in my dream, but when I woke up, I ran to the bathroom mirror to make sure I had a scar instead of a hole.

I'd felt like a foreigner in my own skin, dragging around a sack of muscle and bone held together with medicine. Even after the doctor appointments dwindled and life returned to something that looked like normal, I still hadn't adjusted to being two people in one body, and my wife knew it. She was drifting away like a bottle bobbing in the surf, tide by tide. She wasn't Jessica. She'd never leave, at least not for someone else. But she'd leave with distraction and indifference. And at the thought of the lost intimacy, I felt a blade of ice cold rage so thick I had no room for a reaction or an emotion. My head was clear. The anger had pushed out all the clutter. She was mine to lose, but she was mine.

Three days.

CHAPTER 2.

MONICA

I missed two things.

I missed my freedom, and I missed slavery.

I got myself caught in a nether region where I couldn't come and go as I pleased, and I didn't feel protected.

I was being unfair and I knew it. What man could be expected to keep up Jonathan's intensity for any length of time? No human could continue to be a raging lion after having their heart ripped out.

So, though we burdened each other with many things, I never burdened him with my longing for my dominant Jonathan. That man was gone. I loved the man who replaced him. He was everything I almost lost in that fucking nightmare of a hospital. He was funny and thoughtful. Gracious and wise. He was still the best lover I'd ever laid my hands on.

"Hello?" His voice was thick with sleep. The sun was just coming up over Caracas, tainting the sky brown.

"I'm coming back early," I said as I walked across the tarmac toward the Gulfstream. Jacques waved. His temp copilot for the day took my rolling suitcase and stowed it underneath.

"Really?" Jonathan sounded as awake as a gallon of coffee. "I have something for you."

"But I have to go right into the studio," I said. "Jerry wants me to work on *Forever* for this sampler idea he's—"

"I'm sorry?"

"I'll walk in the door the same time as if I'd stayed here. I just wanted you to know what I was doing with your plane."

7

"Well, thank you."

"Don't be mad."

"Goddess," he said, and I heard something in his voice I hadn't heard in half a year. It stopped me on the steps up to the fuselage door.

"Yes?" I was shocked at the small sound of my own voice.

"I don't give a fuck about the plane."

"It'll be fast. I'll be home by lunch."

"Text me where you're going to be."

"Why?"

"What?"

Fuck. I promised myself I'd never forget what Jessica did to him, yet here I was, serial-bailing on him and giving attitude about it.

"It's the same place as always," I said, backpedalling as I snapped my seatbelt on. "I'm fine."

"Maybe you are," he said, then changed his tone to something more pensive. "Maybe you are."

He hung up and I was left with an oddly-shaped emptiness.

Jonathan loved me. I never questioned that. His love was in everything he did. I heard it in his voice and felt it when he fucked me. Even when he took me like a stranger and reveled in hurting me, there was love in his abandon.

I also didn't question his desire to be married to me, or his commitment in what he thought were the last moments of his life. But they were the last moments. Most couples don't face life and death tests of their love until they're old and grey, or until they had children in middle school, but he and I had been put through the fire unprepared and come out stronger.

Yet, we'd missed the basics, and they weighed on me. I constantly forgot that we loved each other because of the daily misunderstandings and confusions.

"So, I hear you want to get moving on this before Mrs. Drazen goes to Paris?"

I sat next to Jonathan, on his couch, frozen in shock. "Paris? I didn't say I was going?"

"You're going. It's a huge opportunity." He turned back to the agent, who had a decal of a smile across the bottom of her face. "She's the opening act for—"

"Nobody," I interrupted. "I'm not going. So, anyway. No."

The real estate agent's name had been Wendy. Like any real estate agent in Los Angeles, she was perky, perfect coiffed, and blandly unthreatening. She'd come highly recommended for her discretion, her taste, and her ability to manage massive amounts of money seamlessly.

"What kind of house were you looking for?"

"Kind of house?" I'd asked, stalling. Jonathan had been out of the hospital a month and we'd spent it managing a heart transplant. Appointments. Doctors. Medical procedures I didn't understand. Big pills in little boxes. A diet and exercise regiment that made me shudder. And Jonathan himself, my husband, feeling shaky and unsure. I woke up most mornings feeling unqualified to live my life.

"Era," Jonathan had said impatiently. I heard the rasp in his breath. It was late afternoon, and he was going to need to rest. "Something modern. Fifties. I'm sick of leaded glass."

"I, uh—"

"Did you have a neighborhood in mind?" Wendy interrupted me, making eye contact with Jonathan.

"The hills," Jonathan said. "Beechwood, maybe."

"Really, I think the ocean—"

"Great. How many bedrooms? Or do you just want to go by square feet?"

"Big." Jonathan told her. "This house is cramped."

"Cramped?" I interjected. I'd thought his house was palatial, but I'd grown up with eleven hundred square feet, and I didn't like being bulldozed. They both looked at me, and I felt ashamed. And then I'd felt ashamed for feeling ashamed. It wasn't that Jonathan and I disagreed on the style or size of the house that embarrassed me. It was the fact that we hadn't discussed it.

"Wendy, I'm sorry," I'd said, standing. "We're obviously not ready to discuss this. Can we get you to come back some other time?"

"Of course!" she chirped, and was gone in a flutter.

"What was that?" Jonathan asked.

"We're wasting her time until we can come together on something."

He'd looked tired, as usual. He always looked tired in those first months. It had been why I didn't talk to him about anything important. I didn't want to exhaust him. I thought it was the best way to help him get better. Even when I'd missed a period from the combination of stress and depo provera, I didn't tell him because I didn't want to stress him out or start an argument about children.

When he'd gotten back from the hospital, he couldn't really walk. He just didn't have it in him.

He had a staff of people, and a huge family, so he
didn't need me, yet I'd been surprised at how much
he did. He needed to talk, and in those
conversations, he laid our future out like
architectural plans, pointing to the lines and angles
that I needed to see. I rarely disagreed with him. He
was prone to rightful frustration with his body and
the exhaustion of small tasks, and I was still in a
stunned state, functional, competent, and
emotionally dead and broken. I'd thought I was
handling it well. I was the picture of maturity and
capability. I even laughed sometimes, when it
seemed appropriate.

"Children," he'd said, on his back in the bed.
The lights were out, and the flat latte color of the
Los Angeles night sky lit the room. "When can we
start?"

"You mean start having sex again? Your doctor
said any time."

I leaned over him, half-sitting. His bandage had
just been taken off, and the scar on his chest was
still pink.

"Fucking with intention."

"I've never known you to fuck without it."

He smiled and touched my lower lip. "When
does that shot wear off?"

My depo provera shots rendered me infertile
and nearly menstruation free for two to four
months at a time.

"Right after Valentine's I guess."

"No more shots."

"Jonathan, I...I think we should talk about it
again." His expression got wary. I froze, afraid of
upsetting him. "I want children. You have to
understand it's...this is hard to say." I touched his

11

chest, brushing my fingers over the scar. "Everything seems so precarious."

"You'll stop feeling like that. Once I can walk more than ten fucking feet. Soon."

"Let's revisit then. Please. I just need to know you're strong enough to handle running out in the middle of the night for chili chocolate ice cream."

"Who makes that? It sounds disgusting."

"It's delicious."

He pulled me to him, and I laid my head just below his chest. His heart beat in my ear. It sounded perfectly normal, a functioning organ capable of sustaining his body until something else broke. But it wasn't beating with life. It was a ticking clock, and it would stop too soon.

I'd gotten another shot in early February. I reasoned that he didn't need to know. I'd put him off. I knew I couldn't do it much longer, but we were taking it one day, and one white lie at a time.

I hadn't let the shots lapse. But I'd felt something funny, some twitch in my abdomen that was there and not there. A tightness, and I ignored it, then pissed on a stick to make sure. Nada. I'd relaxed, because it was crazy. Depo was 99% effective, and I had another two weeks until I needed another shot.

But it always come up, even when it didn't. When we talked about the house, we needed a bigger room just for the elephant, and after I dismissed Wendy the Realtor, the animal only got bigger.

He'd leaned on the arm of the couch and crossed his ankles, the same posture as the night I'd gone to see him at his office..

"Whatever we get should be the exact opposite of what I got before you were in my life."

"I think that's reactionary."

"That's a big word that means nothing."

"Don't build us on top of what you did or didn't do before. How's that for a definition."

Who were we, standing half a room away from each other with our limbs crossed? How did any of this matter? How did it become important?

If he wanted to pass the next ten years in a big modern house overlooking Los Angeles, who was I to say otherwise? Wasn't that a small price to pay to be with him?

"I want you to go to Paris," he'd said. "You've never been."

"Who's going to watch you? Who's going to make sure you don't forget to do what you're supposed to?"

"If you want children to take care of, that can be arranged."

"I don't."

"Then you don't need to baby me."

And that had been that. We got a house by default. They style he wanted. The location I wanted, because on paper it seemed like a compromise. It had been more of a treaty.

CHAPTER 3.

MONICA

I ate a lunch of chicken fingers and a half a radicchio salad in the engineering room. I shot the shit with Jerry and Deshawn. We talked about promoting the sampler, getting beer thrown at me in Caracas as a sign of respect, the roaches in the hotel, the excellent food. Half an hour later, we were back to work. Executives drifted in and out to hear me. Eddie even showed up for fifteen minutes.

The phone had been face down on the baby grand piano; the sheen of it let me know when the glass lit up with a call or text. But I wouldn't pick it up. I was in the middle of something. Only when I was done did I check it.

—I want to see you—

The text had come ten minutes earlier, when I was in the middle of recording *Forever*. It was based on a poem I'd written while Jonathan was in the hospital, and I was so angry I imagined myself in an eternal, raging battle with death.

I couldn't take a text. We were trying to get the last two words right. *Forever fuck.* It had to sound like a powerful curse, but be muddled, and on key, and gravelly and transcendent, all at the same time. My feet hurt and the foam egg carton pattern on the walls seemed inverted, my brain and eyes were so exhausted.

I couldn't possibly take a text, even from my husband.

—Where are you?—

Ten minutes later.

*—You were supposed to
be out two hours ago—*

I scrolled through his texts. Jerry and the sound team packed up. I was going to have to deal with this. I had my career. He knew what it entailed. He didn't have the right to harass me while I was recording.

I took a deep breath and called him from outside.

"Hi," I said. The parking lot behind the studio smelled like sweaty asshole and stale cigarettes.

"You're out?" Jonathan asked.

"Just finished up."

"I have a surprise for you when you get home."

Home. A house on the beach that already had too many painful memories. Medications. Falls. Fights. He'd been sick and pissed. I loved him. I'd never leave him. But some days, I felt like we were coming apart at the seams.

"The guys were going to dinner. I'm a little hungry."

He paused. The silence seemed eternal, and though I imagined him staring into space with the phone at his ear, when I heard a car door slam, I knew he hadn't been inactive.

"Jonathan, it's—"

"Stay there."

"Not tonight, I—"

"This sounds to me like you're telling me no." The calm, arrogant dominance in his voice was like a slap in the ass because I hadn't heard it in six months. "For the sake of clarity, goddess, when it

15

comes to me, that's not in your vocabulary. I don't hear it."

I said *yes sir* with all the sarcasm of a spoiled adolescent, and immediately regretted it. Luckily, my husband had already hung up the phone.

CHAPTER 4.

JONATHAN

This shit stopped tonight.

I parked in the back and went into the building. There were a couple of doors ajar, behind which I could hear the laughter and mumblings of men. I heard her three down, her voice humming, piano strings getting hammered one by one, slowly.

I slipped into the engineering room and looked at her through the window.

She sat at the keyboard, scribbling something onto a notebook, then considering the keys again, back straight, neck as long and white as a swan's, ebony hair braided and twisted to the top of her head. A goddess. She'd waited. I don't know what would have happened with us if she hadn't.

The engineering booth was empty and dark, and I watched her like a movie. I saw her bite a fingernail. Close her eyes. Tap a finger, then suddenly burst out with a word in one long note. It was *you*. She hit three keys, then three different keys, sang the word again, in a different register, and wrote it down.

It was as if I hadn't seen the length of her neck in months, nor the delicacy of her wrists. I knew every inch of her skin, every curve of her body, yet, that day, when she'd said *no* to me, I anticipated the prospect of showing her why that wasn't going to wash any longer with no little delight.

I went back into the hall, closing the engineering room door behind me.

CHAPTER 5.

MONICA

His scent cut through the dank musk of the studio before the sound of the door closing reached my ears.

"Hi," I said without looking up from my notes. "Can we meet with those guys? Jerry wants to lay out a plan for Wednesday."

His fingertips grazed the back of my neck, and I shuddered, closing my eyes halfway.

"No," he whispered.

"I'll meet you at home later, if you want."

"Stand up."

I looked up. He stood over me, hand at the back of my neck, face broaching no arguments. I don't know what my expression said, but my mind went utterly dark for a second.

I stood, reaching for my bag.

He gently took it from me and laid it back down. I started to object but didn't get past the first syllable before he had his fingers to my lips.

"Unbutton your shirt," he said. We gazed deeply at each other for longer than usual, and I knew even before my fingers touched my shirt, that he wasn't interested in a standard, sweet, encounter.

He brushed his thumb over my lips, across my jaw, and lodged it under my chin, fording me to look at the dusty fluorescent lights.

I undid my buttons in a businesslike fashion while he spoke.

"I haven't told you this in a long time, so I want to remind you. You are mine. Any time. Any place. Without questions. You get on your knees when I say. You spread your legs when I say. You open

18

your mouth and take whatever I put in it. Do you understand?"

He must have felt me swallow against the heel of his hand. He was back. I didn't know when or how, but this wasn't sick Jonathan getting pissed at his handful of pills. This wasn't the guy who let me top him, or the man who made love to me fearfully and gently. That man was a good husband. Difficult, because he felt like his body wasn't his own, but a good life mate by any standard.

For as long as I'd been married, I hadn't felt safe.

Until then, staring at the ceiling, unprepared to hear the voice of my king again. Then, my insides vibrated like a piano string and I shut my eyes tight against tears.

"Yes, sir," I said.

"Pull your pants down."

I worried about the door. Was it open? And the door to the engineering room. Anyone could walk in.

This was a simple matter of trust, which I'd forgotten how to do. *Trust him. You're safe with him.*

I opened my pants and wiggled them down. I wore lace and garter, which felt scratchy and uncomfortable under jeans, but I wore it because I promised I would, even if I'd promised a different man.

He slipped his finger under the straps. His touch had gone electric, exactly right, like when we first met. I felt it through layers of skin and muscle, to my bones.

"All the way off."

I stepped out of my pants.

"Why are you crying, goddess?"

"I don't know."

"What's your safe word?"

I blurted a laugh to the ceiling. "Fuck. I forgot."

"Do you want a new one?" He slid his finger under my bra, pushing it up, releasing my breasts. The nipples were hard candies, ready for him.

"Yes, sir."

"Your choice."

"Invictus."

He pinched a nipple and pulled it to the point of delicious pain. "Out of the night that covers me, black as the pit from pole to pole, I thank whatever gods may be, for my unconquerable soul."

"Jonathan…" His name was a prayer.

"Turn around."

I faced the piano, putting my back to him. He slid his hand over my neck and around my shirt collar, pulling it down my arms, drawing his hands over my skin.

"I'm going to ask you something," he said, pulling my long sleeves halfway off. He twisted the sleeves around my arms, wrapping them around and tying them tightly at the elbows.

His pause long enough for me to say, "sir?"

"Are you happy?" he asked. I heard the distinct clack of his belt buckle.

I didn't answer. He slid his belt out of his pants with a *whook*.

"I asked you a question."

"Yes, sir."

"Is that the answer?" He gripped the back of my neck

"It's confirmation that I heard you."

With a sharp push, he pinned my face to the shiny black of the piano.

"Are you happy?" he repeated.

"Can you be more specific?"

"Sure." With a thwack that was as hard as it was unexpected, he slapped my ass with his belt. I screamed.

"Too hard?"

"No, sir." It was. A fierce burn was settling where he'd hit me, and I already wanted more. I wanted him to tear me apart. In the second, the breath's worth of time it took for my body to register pain, I cracked. I didn't want to go to dinner with Jerry and the guys and I didn't want to go home. I wanted to hurt, and hurt deep. I wanted to feel pain, and safety, and surrender; to lose myself and my own will. I'd forgotten how much I needed it, but like a woman waking from a dreamless sleep, the reality of who I was came back to me. I swore I wouldn't say my safe word until I was near death.

"Behave, then, before I gag you." He whacked me again, and again. I grunted, but didn't cry out, even when he hit the sensitive area at the backs of my thighs.

"Now," his breath rasped with effort. "Tell me, goddess, are you happy?" his last stroke was so hard it felt like a blowtorch on my ass. He took the hair on the back of my head in his fist and brought his face close to mine. "To avoid misunderstandings. Are you *happily married?*"

I swallowed.

He put his belt down in front of my face and squeezed my ass. The pain was overwhelming. I could barely see through it, nor could I form words past the gushing arousal between my legs.

"Answer me," he said. "And the truth. Are you happy?"

He was foggy through my tears, but his voice was clear enough to focus on.

"No," I said. "I'm not."

21

As much as I broke down into tears and hitched sobs, he seemed unfazed by the news. As if he'd already known. And as if he didn't give a shit about my happiness. He brought his hand over my burning cheeks, lacing a finger in the crack, down to my opening.

I was soaked. Dripping. Gushing readiness for him. I wished he'd asked me for the truth after he fucked me, because how could he now? I tell him I'm miserable and expect a body-ripping, passionate screw? Crazy, magical thinking.

He slipped a finger inside me. I'd fucked him a hundred times in the past six months, but that finger cruelly jamming into me, with the palm laying against my scalding ass, was the best thing I'd had in half a year.

"Thank you for telling me the truth," he said. "But you're wet. And crying."

"I'm sorry, sir."

"Poor goddess." He pulled his finger out and slipped it to the hard nodule of my clit. My eyes shut. My mouth opened. My cunt was awake with anticipation as he continued. "Even in love, you need pain."

"I love you," I whispered.

He drew his hand back and slapped my ass with full force. I bit back a cry. "Don't talk," he growled. "There's been wholly too much talking between us, and not nearly enough."

I nodded.

He folded the belt in two and said, "Open your mouth." When I did, he put the belt in it. "Bite."

I bit the leather. It was still warm from hitting me. Had he ever been this cruel and hard? Had he ever been this *dominant*? I couldn't remember. I couldn't think.

Then Jonathan put his hands on my hips, and let his cock touch where I was wet. I bit the belt as if I wanted to swallow it. He didn't ask for permission to jam his dick into me in one fell stroke, making me grunt into the tanned skin. He didn't ask if my happiness was required. He just fucked me. He fucked me like I wasn't even there, slapping himself against my burning ass cheeks, a frame of pain for the pleasure between my legs. He pulled my cheeks apart, stretching them, pain everywhere, and drove into me with everything he had, using me mercilessly. I lost myself in him, in the hurt, the rising tide of my emotions. I'd told him I was unhappy, and the weight of the misery fell off me, leaving an empty place for him to fill with his cock and his searing belt.

I grunted with every thrust. It was coming. The rush of pleasure. My grunts turned to squeals, and he slowed to barely moving.

"I didn't say you could come."

I hadn't had to ask permission for an orgasm in six months. I hadn't even thought of it.

He removed the belt.

"I'm sorry, sir," I gasped. "May I come?"

"When?"

"Now?" I paused for a hitched breath. "And later, if it pleases you."

"No." He slowed, letting me feel every inch of him. He opened my cheeks again, right where my legs met my ass and I was red and sore, getting his whole length in.

I choked out a half sob, half moan.

"No," he said, slapping my ass. "The answer is still no."

"I don't think I can stop it."

He pulled out. I gasped. But as much as I expected him to continue fucking me, I didn't expect what he did next, quickly guiding himself to my asshole and mercilessly pushing forward.

"No!" I shouted.

He yanked my head back by the hair. "What?"

I couldn't repeat it. Safeword or no, he'd stop, and I knew, more than anything that I didn't want him to stop. "Nothing. Please, go on."

He pushed the rest of his cock in my ass without preamble, my soft weeping turned into face-soaking sobs. "God, oh God it hurts."

"Pain is the point, isn't it?"

"Yes, sir."

"Your ass is mine, whether I warn you or not. Do you understand?"

"Yes."

He yanked my hair again, pulling back until I faced him. "Yes, what?"

"Yes, sir."

The first few strokes were murder. I felt torn apart, ripped from the inside. We'd done some gentle, well-lubricated anal in the past few months. But not like this. Not as a beating.

"You've been a bitch, goddess. That's over. From now on, you step when I say walk. You eat when I feed you. You come when I allow it. If I so much as look at your knees, you get on them and open your fucking mouth."

I grunted. He reached around me and put his palm to my throat. He pulled me back, and though I felt like I was falling, I trusted him and put weight on my aching legs, shifting back. He sat on the piano bench, and with my back to his front and his cock in my ass, I sat into him.

"Spread your legs." Not giving me a chance to even obey, he yanked my legs apart, squeezing my ass cheeks together, tightening me around his cock. I bit back a cry of pain. "All the way. I want your cunt out."

I spread my knees, on tiptoes to the floor, fighting for balance. My elbows were still tied behind my back, and when it looked like I'd fall, he pulled me upright.

"Reach back," he said. "Spread those gorgeous cheeks apart."

I did, fighting the constraints of my knotted shirt, cursing the stinging skin on my ass as much as I blessed it.

"Now, come down, all the way. All the way. That's it. Bury me in you." He reached around and slipped his middle finger in my cunt, gathering wetness, and dragging it to my clit. "You're not coming until I say. And you're going to hold back by concentrating on one thing, and one thing only."

"What, sir?" I groaned, the pleasure in my clit pushing against the pain behind it.

"Pleasing me. So. Fuck. And fuck hard. Go."

I moved up his length, and back down, his shaft sliding against my anus, friction hot against the dry muscle.

"Faster."

His cock beat my insides, shredded me, while his fingers took my cunt three at a time and the heel of his hand kept a constant pressure on my clit.

"Come on, goddess. I'm not pleased."

I grabbed my cheeks wider, slammed down on him harder, knees aching, arms on fire, ass beyond pain. Yet the pleasure between my legs grew, pressing against the agony and winning.

"That's good," he growled. "Very good."

"Thank you." I gasped, relieved, relaxed now because he was content. I heard his breaths getting shorter. I was close, but I didn't care. I wanted him to have what he wanted. I wanted him to be satisfied. I beat down on his cock, mindless of what I was doing to myself.

"I'm going to come," he said.

"Thank you," I squeaked, more tears streaming.

"Come with me."

"Yes. Oh, yes."

He grunted, but it was more than a grunt, and in the second before I lost myself in pleasure I noted how vocal he was. More than ever. He released, truly, fully, losing control, pulling my hair until I thought he'd tear it out. I was washed away in it, the pleasure of his hand on my clit, the torture in my ass as my orgasm clenched it around his cock in an undulating rhythm. I came forever, lost in it, in him, his satisfaction, in the pain. I was gone, my identity washed away in complete submission to his pleasure and his will; without ambition or desire of my own, simply enslaved, caged, collared. Nothing. No one. Not a feeling of dissatisfaction in my belly, only humility and a feeling of complete, overwhelming gratitude.

"Goddess?" he whispered when I stopped twitching.

I tried to answer, but I was blubbering. I took a few breaths to calm down. "Yes, sir?"

"Are you okay?"

"Thank you."

He untied me. I put my aching arms on my knees and he pushed me gently forward, his dick slipping out of my ass. I sucked in a breath.

He pulled me into his lap and kissed the tears running down my cheeks. I held him and wept fully.

26

The emotional release poured out of me as he rubbed my back and kissed my face and neck. My awareness of the world around me, my body, the chair, the room, the building, the time of day, was brought about by the softness of his lips and the way he whispered my name, *goddess, goddess, goddess.*

"I haven't been what you need," he said softly.

"You couldn't be. I understand."

"That's over now."

"Thank you."

He put his hands on my cheeks and brushed my lashes with his thumbs. I let my eyes flutter closed.

"You can't leave me until I destroy you."

"If you destroy me, I'll never leave."

"Regularly." He took out a monogrammed hankie and held it up. "Blow."

I blew my nose. He pinched and wiped for me, as if I were a child.

He kissed my lips, taking them against his, owning them with tenderness and confidence. I let his tongue into my mouth, its soothing warmth, exploring me as if for the first time. The tenderness with which he kissed me was in such contrast to the beating I'd just received, that I broke down in tears again. He held me and rocked me in the soundproof studio for what seemed like hours, saying sweet things in my ear. I felt so good, so calm, so loved.

"You'd better cancel dinner," he said. "You're going to need some serious after care."

"You think the guys would notice if I ate standing up?"

"Come home, and I'll feed you in bed."

"Yes, Jonathan. Yes to everything."

"And you shall have everything."

CHAPTER 6.

MONICA

Sometimes, I felt like I wasn't in love with a man. Sometimes, when things were tense, or we fought, or we made love, or I was away too long or in the house too many weeks, sometimes when we disagreed, or even when he kissed me on the back patio, I stopped seeing him as a man. I stopped seeing him as even human. I felt as though I'd married a time bomb.

Which, if I gave it a moment's more thought on the plane to some dipshit town or on the way to a meeting, he was more human in that ticking time bombness than if he'd been a normal man with a normal heart. More human in his mortality, his vulnerability, his lack of control.

Wives care for sick husbands who come back from war. Husbands stand beside wives with illnesses that deteriorate them body and mind. We read about their strength and dedication, their stand-by-your-manness. No one talks about the adjustments and the sacrifices. Grieving for the husband who doesn't exist any more isn't feelgood news. We're supposed to be chipper and upbeat and never admit to a single soul that we missed the men we thought we married.

I felt like a piece of shit for missing the hard, bruising sex. It was different with Gabby. When I wanted to go out, but had to watch her, I felt burdened. I admitted it to myself, but did what I had to do anyway. I always felt like shit about that too. With Jonathan, I still so ecstatic he was alive I didn't even realize how much I'd missed him until he asked me if I was happy.

"What's wrong?" Jonathan asked in the back of the Bentley. He'd just fucked my ass raw in the studio, just hurt me badly, and I'd begged him for every stroke. I'd never felt closer to him than in those minutes of pain. But on the way back, after I came down from my high and we had a bathroom break. I remembered why the last six months had been so hard.

"Nothing."

He stroked my arm with his fingertips. Perfect pressure for the gathering of electricity, as always. "Nothing?"

I shook my head, more at myself than at his disbelief. Nothing, my ass. Something. Everything.

"That was a lot of exertion, back there."

Exertion wasn't just a word, but a keyword. Code for unreasonable fear. Secret speak for death. Terror in a few breaths of syllables and the tongue rubbing on the back of the teeth.

"You've been told a hundred times—"

"I know, please." I dismissed him. "I know."

He grabbed a fistful of hair on the back of my neck and turned me to face him, and my scalp became a center of pleasure. "You're shutting down."

I couldn't deny him the truth. Not after he'd torn me open. For those minutes in the studio, when he commanded me, I forgot to worry about him, and he was again my master and king. And when he pulled my hair I wanted to be ripped apart again, just for the release from thinking about him dying.

"I'm not," I said. "I'm just—"

"Open your legs."

I was pissed he'd ask at a time like this, and relieved. I spread my legs across the leather seat.

Not enough for him, apparently, because he pulled my head back and yanked my knees farther apart. I gasped when a bullet of arousal shot through me.

He pressed four fingers between my legs, where the panels of my jeans met.

"I am not going to die fucking you." He scratched the fabric, and I felt the tease through the layers.

Was this the time to answer honestly? Shouldn't we talk over dinner, or in bed? Or across a desk surrounded by pens and blotters and serious things?

"You might. You could."

"I won't." He pushed against my crotch and I pushed back at him as if I had no control over my body.

"You might," I gasped when he undid my jeans. "And you deny it and it's a lie you tell yourself. And I'm tired of walking around and pretending it's not a problem, because it is. It's a big problem. It's all I think about."

He slid his hand past my waistband until the tip of his middle finger reached my

clit. He barely pressed on it, just rotated around the slip of skin at the top.

"You never told me that."

"I have to be strong for you. Because you chase me out of the house to work, and I think it's because you don't want me to see you weak. And, oh God, Jonathan, I'm going to come."

"No, you're not." He reduced pressure and intensity, until I could only feel the outer edge of his hand's heat. "Pull your shirt up. Let me see your tits."

I yanked up the shirt and bra, and he leaned down and sucked on a nipple so hard and fast it hurt like hell. I bucked under him.

"I'm going to die before you," he said, taking a last nip before putting his face to mine. "Way before you. You want to spend the time worrying? Or fucking?"

Which? Was that the only choice? This dichotomy of soul eating pain or soul revealing pleasure. I waited too long to answer, apparently, because he circled his fingertip over my clit again, barely touching it. I groaned. I wanted to say fucking, to tell him what he wanted to hear, but when he had me like this, I couldn't tell one of the thousand untruths about my feelings. I couldn't say what would make him happy for the sake of saving him from stress.

"Which is it, goddess?"

"I'm going to come."

He brought his finger down my folds, to where I was wettest, leaving my clit kissed by nothing but the damp air in my jeans, bringing the rest of me to life. His outer fingers touched the welts he'd left earlier, setting them on fire.

"Which is it?" he asked.

"Fuck me or let me come," I whispered. He pulled his hand out of my pants. The loss was painful. "You are not stopping," I groaned. "Don't even…"

He took my face in his hands, putting his nose to mine. "You only talk when your cunt lets you. From now on, I control when you talk. And today, you talk."

The car stopped in front of our house and the gate clanged closed behind us.

"You're a son of a bitch." My body arched toward him, making a lie of my words.

"Before I was in the hospital, you could hold yourself together. Now you're calling me a son of a bitch for doing what it's my right to do."

I glared at him, hating him and loving him at the same time, pain and pleasure always hand in hand with my king.

"Button up," he said, pulling my shirt down. I closed the fly on my jeans and he opened the door. The late afternoon sun blasted my face, turning Lil's form into a rectangular silhouette.

We didn't speak as we walked to the house. A modest thing by Drazen standards, it had a private beach in the back, and the whole of Malibu in front, an old house built at the crest of the modern era by an ambitious architect who was way ahead of his time. It didn't have a porch, but a small overhang shading the wide front door. He disabled the security system and put his hand on the knob, but didn't turn it.

Lil drove away, the sound of the engine giving way to the evensong birds and the breath of the freeways below.

I started to think about everything I could be doing. My brain chemistry had changed in the past six months, and when upset, the new rhythm of my thoughts went to music and the business of making it. One ass fuck in the studio wasn't going to change that.

"Come on. I have things to do," I said, knowing it wasn't going to go over well. I reveled in my defiance. Fuck him with his new heart and old ways. If he wanted to talk he could take me to dinner.

He swung the door open, but didn't leave room for me to pass.

I crossed my arms. He smirked. I felt the tightening of my cheeks as I almost smirked with him. What game was I playing? I wanted to get to work, and I wanted him to fuck me.

No, I didn't want him to fuck me. I wanted him to either rip me apart or let me make music mourning the loss of my wounds. If this defaulted to a vanilla middle ground because he thought he'd made his point, I was going to lose my shit.

"Take your clothes off. All of them."

I rolled my eyes. Lightning quick, like a man who had done nothing but work on his reflexes for the past six months, he grabbed a handful of my hair and dragged me to my knees. My safe word was *Invictus* and I probably still had a tangerine option. But the insides of my thighs tingled when he leaned down and growled in my ear.

"Unbutton your shirt."

I reached for my placket and carefully, without fumbling, undid the buttons one by one.

"I'll do what I have to to get you to talk to me," he said. "So first…" he yanked my hair and I gasped. "Take it off. And the bra."

I shook both off until I was bare-breasted at the front door. How would he get my pants off? What did he intend?

He let go of my hair.

"Stand up."

I got on my feet. He stood in the doorway, framed by a house I'd agreed to with a shrug, hands at his sides. One of his fingers twitched.

I crossed my arms. "Are we going in or not?" I asked, leaning on one hip, breasts out as if I didn't give a shit one way or the other how naked I was. "I'm tired and my ass hurts, can we just—"

"You're really pushing it."

I tapped a single finger on my bicep, a tic of impatience. Even though his beautiful green eyes didn't leave mine, I knew he saw it, and even if his mouth didn't smile, I knew I was pleasing him. We needed this, and we needed it to go down exactly the way it was going to go down.

He put a finger on my lower lip. "Open your mouth."

I didn't.

With his other hand he cupped my jaw and exerted pressure, slowly opening my mouth. God, I wanted his cock in it. I wanted to taste the soft skin as it slid to the back of my throat. I relaxed my mouth, and he put his fingers in. First one, then four, pressing my tongue down. He pulled me to him, speaking softly and firmly into my face.

"I don't mind repeating myself. This is my mouth, and when I say open it, it opens."

I couldn't speak, but my eyes agreed. I was putty in his hands.

"Get your pants off while I explain my position."

I unbuttoned and unzipped while he held my jaw open. I couldn't swallow, and drool formed over his fingers.

"Do you remember the hospital? The week before the first surgery?"

Remember? How could I forget? I got heart palpitations thinking about it. Any time I smelled alcohol or something beeped my chest felt as if it had been encased in a clenched fist.

"That week we had rules," he said. "Should I remind you?"

I nodded as much as I could.

"Get your pants down."

I wiggled, slid them down, while he spoke. "The rules were: only the truth, even if it hurt. We would never protect each other from each other. And no judgment."

I got my pants down to my knees. I was twisted, fighting the tight jeans, the pressure of his fingers, and the memory of lying next to him in the neverdark of Sequoia Hospital.

He removed his hand, which was wet with spit, dripping down his arm to the elbow.

"All the way off."

I leaned to get my shoes off. He held me by the elbow when I almost fell, then resumed watching the clumsy and twisted operation until I was completely naked before him. He was perfectly calm, perfectly commanding. Only the huge bulge in his pants betrayed how involved he was in what was happening.

I stood with my hands at my sides.

"I remember," I said.

"I want that again."

"It's hard when you're telling me to get my clothes off."

"You know what, Monica, you don't even know yourself. Look at you. I haven't seen you this relaxed in months. The only time you let your worry go is when you give me control. And your worry is what keeps you from being honest."

I swallowed. Blinked. A torrent of wetness welled behind my eyes, "I don't want to break the scene."

"Stay still. Stay naked. Speak your mind."

"I almost died with you a hundred times. That recovery room, they had you in this induced coma and you looked dead. There were bags of blood. Bags, hanging over you and you were all opened up. And, I'm sorry, I haven't said this because you're the one who went through it." I swallowed a gallon of tears. "I don't want to see you like that again. But I think about it all the time. I dream about it. I see it when I close my eyes. I want you to live, so I do what I think is going to make you happy and I always get it wrong. Stay or go. I give you attention or none. It's always wrong."

"What about your happiness?"

"It doesn't matter. Not as much as yours. It's not life or death."

"It is, Monica. It is."

I shook my head. "You can't convince me of that. We can do this hurtful honesty thing all day. You're the priority and I'm okay with that. Deal with it."

He nodded, looking down for a blink, then up at me. He reached for my wrists.

"These go behind your back."

I did as instructed.

"Now, get on your knees."

I bent them. With my hands behind my back, it was hard to balance.

"Do you need some help?" he asked.

"Yes."

I thought he'd take me gently by the elbow, but dragged me down. He was right. I was relaxed, totally submitting and trusting him, loving every bit of discomfort he dished out.

"Spread your knees apart."

I did, too slowly for him. He kicked them wide.

"Do you remember your safeword?" He asked, unbuckling his belt.

"Yes." A tingling rush went down my spine with the promise of his dominance and the way it made me forget how fragile he really was.

His cock was out in the next second. "Open. Your. Mouth."

I parted my lips enough to breathe, and before I could open my throat or prepare, he put his cock between them and pushed my head into him. I choked on the mass of it, but the scent of soap, the taste of skin, the shape and thrust of him brought a wave of pleasure, and a strong desire to please him.

"Take it, Goddess. Take it all. Not one inch should be left."

He pushed forward again, fucking my face mercilessly. He pulled out, letting me breathe, making eye contact from above. Checking on me. I was safe. I gasped, chest heaving, and opened my mouth again.

"I want you to think about something," he said. "While I take your mouth, I want you to think about how its purpose is my pleasure. To fuck." He stuck his dick down my throat, all of it in one stroke, pulling it out as violently as he'd put it in. "To talk," he jammed it in again, before I could utter a word. "Whatever I say."

He began in earnest, treating my throat the way he'd treated my ass an hour before, as a receptacle for his soap-scented cock, moving my head by my hair, pulling out to let me breathe, but no longer than necessary. My hands behind me, I couldn't wipe the drool off my chin or move my hair from my face.

"I'm going to come down your throat," he said.

He was so strong, so solid, so commanding with a wisp of hair over his forehead, his monster cock dripping with my spit, hanging in the foreground of my vision.

"You're going to swallow every fucking drop," he said. "Do you understand?"

I opened my mouth as wide as I could, looking up at him through my hair. I wanted to tell him to fuck me anywhere he wanted. To make it hurt. Make it uncomfortable. I wanted to forget everything in our way. The hurt, the stress, the worry, I wanted to break the cycle again, and be nothing more than under him.

But he didn't give me a chance to beg for it. He cupped my jaw in his other hand and stuck his wet cock in my waiting mouth, fucking my throat. He could live forever. He could pound my face like this in an eternal grind, never sick, never dying, never at risk. No. This dominant beast was built to fuck and to hurt and to live.

He pulled out long enough to let me breathe and then shoved it back in, coming with a bark, his balls pulsing against my lower lip. His hair-pulling violence turned to stroking and caressing as he filled my throat, slipping out for a breath, and sliding in again.

"Goddess," he whispered. "Mine mine mine…"

My arms and knees ached. My throat was sore. Thank god I didn't have to sing the next day. Not that he'd care. This Jonathan, my Jonathan, with his come coating the walls of my throat as I swallowed, looking up at him. He smiled down at me, and when he picked me up and carried me though the door, I forgot to worry about him at all.

CHAPTER 7.

JONATHAN

I could see this was going to take some time. It took me months to figure out we even had a problem, it wouldn't take me that much less to solve.

The flip side of the loyalty I loved was her stubbornness. She'd fully engaged in her submission when we started out because it was new and exciting. She'd discovered things she didn't know about herself, and she'd watched me discover my own boundaries as well as hers. Then I got sick, and her world flipped. Now she was distrustful, and to her, the stakes were life and death.

All this made me want to fuck her harder, to drive submission back into her. While my dick was out, she was obedient and subservient, perfect as usual. In the doorway of our house, her mouth open, her chin slick with spit, waiting for me to come down her throat, she was a goddess. But once this was over, she was going to close her mouth and not talk about what was bothering her. She was going to simmer, and worry and seethe, holding it all inside in an effort to protect me.

It was cute. Sweet, even. In a way, her protectiveness made me love her more than I thought I could love anyone. She was a mother lion, even with her hands behind her back and her mascara running down her cheeks.

I laid her on the bed. It faced the Pacific ocean, and the constant crash of the waves was going to make a nice backdrop over her screams of pleasure. She'd wanted to live on the beach, and I'd given her that, but I'd never given her myself. That was going to change. I couldn't live like this.

39

And as if cued, I had a vision as I carried her. In four-dimension Technicolor, unbidden, clear as reality and sharper than the truth: My heart blew through the scar in my chest, and I dropped her. The vision went *whoosh* when the heart flew out of me, *thup* when it landed on the floor, and *clonk* when I dropped her. I didn't hear myself fall, because I was dead.

This had to stop, but I didn't know how to do it. I didn't know how to shut it down. I shook myself free of the afterburn as I laid her on the bed.

"I missed you," she said, and I knew what she meant.

"You barely knew me." I rolled her onto her stomach. She tucked her hands under her thighs.

"How much do I need to know you to love you?"

"Put your hands on the headboard," I said, pulling her hair from her face. She stretched her arms and turned to face the big glass doors onto the patio. The beach on the other side was private, and that slice of sunset was ours alone. Her eyes were blasted light brown in the dying sun, and they followed me as I stepped back and looked at her.

She was long, and beautiful, with hair like a turbulent ocean on her back. She was my songbird, my goddess, my slice of control in a world of chaos.

Ten years with her was better than sixty with anyone less.

I picked her legs up by the ankles and bent the knees, spreading them apart. Her cunt was wet and her ass was welted pink. Looking back up at her face, her eyes closed tightly, the wrinkles in the skin around the wet lashes, I remembered how hard I'd hit her. Six months worth of frustration. I'd never hit her out of anger, only arousal, but maybe the two had gotten mixed up somewhere.

"This hurts," I said, hovering my hand over her ass.

"Yes," she said, eyes open into the sun again. "Thank you."

She wasn't trained to thank me for spankings. No one had told her it was how a submissive was supposed to please their master. She simply thanked me because she'd gotten something from me she couldn't give to herself. How could I not love her?

"Wait here." I kissed her cheek and went to the bathroom, snapping open the medicine cabinet. I had a shaving salve and a lubricant. Abandoned hair things. Toothpaste. Band-aids. Monica had a pale pink box of who-even-knew under the sink. The movers had taken everything and brought it from my house to this new house, and my wife and I had been too distracted and too vanilla to stock anything we needed for her poor, welted ass. I'd been a sorry excuse of a dominant.

I laughed at myself and put the lubricant back. That wasn't going to work. I guessed I was within my rights to check Monica's little pink box. We were married, after all, and it was for her own good.

I snapped it open. Little half used tubes of whatnot clacked around. Perfumey stuff that would burn. Zinc oxide would be fine for a small area but this was a whole bottom that needed attention. I clicked open a smaller box. Ah. Sunburn ointment and Neosporin. Perfect. I checked a little velvet bag with a drawstring. I didn't know what I was hoping for, maybe the home-run of ass lotions, or a magic unguent that would make her able to sit for more than five minutes without flinching. I just opened it and slid out the white plastic stick. A pregnancy test.

41

I didn't have a nerve to my heart, so I couldn't feel it stop and seize up. Couldn't feel the squeeze in my chest. But I knew it was there.

I turned the plastic wand. Not breathing. Not thinking about the fact that I'd been snooping in something that had been inside a bag, inside a box, inside a cabinet.

One line.

Not pregnant.

I wasn't relieved. I wasn't disappointed. I just realized how much I wanted there to be two lines, and how little control I had over it.

I slapped everything back in its place and went into the bedroom. She was still there, face down, hands touching the headboard, bathed in the sunset. It would be dark in a few minutes, so I turned on the little lamp by the bed.

"I found these in your stuff," I said, holding out the tubes.

"I think the neosporin's expired."

I flipped the tube. "Next month."

"Yes, sir."

I sat on the edge of the bed. "Ass up."

She shifted, arching just enough to get her pelvis off the bed.

"Goddess, when I say ass up, I mean ass up." I put my hand under her and jacked her up until her ass was in the air. She groaned. I spread her legs under her and pressed down her lower back. Perfect.

I kissed a raw welt and she squeaked in pain.

"None of that," I said, and though my words were cruel, I didn't want her to hurt right then. She'd earned her pleasure.

I squeezed a lump of the sunburn cream onto my finger. It was cool to the touch, and when I put it on the pink skin, she breathed easily.

"Now," I said. "We have a problem. Fucking you in the ass isn't going to solve it."

"Yes, sir."

"First off. We need to drop the sirs and thank yous and all that shit until I say otherwise. We're off scene. Verbally. The ass stays up or I'll welt your welts."

"Fine."

"I want you to talk to me." I dragged a mound of clear cream over the curve of her ass, watching it get smaller in the seam between she and I, disappearing into a cool coat.

"I'm fine," she said. "Everything is fine. I think, just...I think I needed this. What you're giving me now."

I ran my fingers on the inside of her thigh until there was no cream on them, and slipped my middle finger between her legs. Her eyes fluttered closed.

"You're not fine. You're wet as fuck,." I put my fingertip on her clit. "You're so close I shouldn't even touch you. But fine? You're not fine."

"I am. I—"

"You don't tell your husband you're not happy and an hour later tell him you're fine because he fucked you hard enough."

I slid two fingers inside her. Wet wasn't a word to describe her. She tightened around me, and my dick stretched my pants. I pulled my hand out, running it over her clit again, front to back, touching every surface, waking it up.

"Jonathan, I can't talk to you like this."

"You don't talk to me, period."

"I want to come."

"You'll come." I gingerly spread her ass cheeks. She looked like she'd been fucked by a battering ram. The bruises were rising already, and she was deep red around the edges. I'd need to leave that part of her alone for awhile. "Tell me," I said, kissing her lower back while stroking between her legs. "Tell me how it's been for you."

"I don't want to. I don't want to upset you. I just want you to be okay."

"I am okay, except that you've been closed to me." I put three fingers in her, and she bucked. "Stay still. You can take your hands off the headboard." She tucked them under her. I slowly removed my fingers. "Tell me one thing you think of that makes you worry." She sighed. I put my hands on her thighs and kissed her clit. "Tell me."

"I love you."

"That's not what I asked."

She paused. "And I wonder if you've taken your rejection meds."

"I know you've been checking the bottles."

"When I'm here."

"Exactly." I gave her a long stroke with my tongue. She groaned, but stayed still. Such a good woman.

"I told you I'd stop travelling if you wanted."

"I don't want."

"Why?" I sucked her clit because it tasted good, and because I wanted to please her, but mostly, because I didn't know how to answer her question. She'd just accepted my encouragement and never asked why it was there. I felt the muscles of her thighs tremble and tighten, and as if she spoke best on the edge of orgasm, and continued. "You throw me away. We have such a short time together and you kick me out. Jonathan, if you don't want me, let

44

me go. Don't stay out of obligation. Not for ten years of misery with me."

I pulled my face away. "Oh, God Monica. You can't mean that."

I'd intended to torment her for as long as it took, then bring her to orgasm with my tongue until she begged me to stop. But she broke me with those words, and I changed the plan. I got on my knees and pushed her onto her back.

Her hair made a ladder across her face, and I brushed it away. Her eyes were wet, and her face was creased from being pressed to the sheets.

"I mean it," she said. "That heart has ten years in it and you can't spend them with the wrong person just because you got married under pressure. It's wrong."

"Would you have married me if I'd asked you under any other circumstances? If I'd taken you up to Mulholland and asked you under the stars, with a ring and a few nice words?"

"I would have said yes."

"Why?"

"I love you is why. But that doesn't mean you're obligated. Because you wouldn't have asked. Not for awhile."

I must have had a look on my face, or made a sound that hit a button, because she blinked, and tears ran down the side of her face. "I'm not trying to make it about me. And I'm not looking for reassurance. But if you deny it…"

"I'm not denying it. I would have asked you…I don't know when. After a few birthdays. There are no rules for the way it happened."

"I want you to think about it," she said.

"About what?"

"About if this is what you really want." Her voice was sober and cold. "If I'm what you really want to be married to."

"Goddess."

"No. I mean it. If you want to be together, but not married. I just want you to have what you want. I want you to be sure."

I almost answered. I almost reassured her and told her how I felt about her. I almost made metaphors with the sky and stars, weaving threads of certainty into a gauze of confidence. But even if I got her to believe it for a second, she'd wake up in the morning wondering if I'd lied to appease her.

So I kissed her cheek. "Will you stay?"

She nodded, and I felt the insecurity in it. She'd never been insecure with me, and it unmoored me at the same time as it filled me with a feeling I hadn't had in a long time.

I unbuttoned my shirt. She reached up and helped me, pulling it off and throwing it across the room. I got my pants off and stood over her naked body. Her magnificent tits were goosebumped, nipples hard, skin golden in the lamplight.

"Spread your legs for me." She did it, hitching her knees up. There was so much between us. I would have married her in an instant, under any circumstances, and as I wedged myself between her legs, I knew my job wasn't to reassure her with pretty words or gifts, but with actions. She'd believe it or I'd die trying.

I put her hands over her head and leaned on them. "Look at me."

Her eyes went wide, looking up. "May I come?"

I pushed against her, going to the rhythm of slow torture. "Quiet now, Goddess. Don't ask again."

Her face went from pleasure to constricted concentration as she tried not to come. I fucked her harder. She pleaded with me without saying a word. Her face begged for release, her beauty crunched into pain.

"Say my name," I said.

"Jonathan."

"Monica."

"Jonathan." She cried it, sobbed, breaking herself into pieces to say it.

"Come, my wife. Come for me."

She came in two strokes, arching and twisting. I held myself back until she finished, drinking in every cry, every moment, every shudder.

My purpose in life had been simple up until then. Live. Just live. Now I had a resolution. Love her until she believed it.

CHAPTER 8.

Love was easy. Love, the way everyone else defined it, was the fun part. But every hell, every conflict, every bit of miserable anxiety in those first six months had been born of nothing but love. I'd thought that was my new life. Ten years of it at least, until his heart gave out and he had to find another. Then another ten. Or more. Or less. Or not. Or maybe. I was playing Russian roulette with God by being away so much, but I thought he wanted me away, and he thought I wanted to be away. I didn't know whether to jump or crawl those first six months, and then he came to the studio and fucked me like an animal.

The morning after he reclaimed me, with my ass aching and my cunt as sore as it had ever been, I woke up forgetting to wonder about his pills and his life. Just for a second. And in that crack in my wall of concern, bled something else I hadn't thought about since Sequoia. It needled me every time I saw Declan, and disappeared behind the buzz of death seconds after Jonathan's father was out of the room. Now that I thought of it in his arms with the sound of the ocean outside, I couldn't go another second without telling him, even if it meant it was our last together.

His eyes were closed, light lashes casting darker shadows. His chest rose and fell under me, and his scar was hard white beneath my hand.

"Jonathan," I whispered, hoping he was asleep.

"Yes," he answered clearly, eyes still shut, as if he was wide awake and had been listening to my thoughts the entire time. I got my knees under me, the pain of every movement a reminder of how many times he'd brutalized me the night before, and how consistently I'd begged for it.

"I need to tell you something."

He opened his eyes. Had they always been that green? Or was it a trick of the light and my fear of losing him?

"Okay, go ahead." He reached out and stroked the top of my breast. I pulled his hand away and held it in my lap. I paused. A hundred years passed, and he said nothing. Not a word of encouragement or doubt. I could have hung myself in the amount of time he'd wait. As always, he was a patient man in all things.

"When you were, I mean you weren't yourself," I started, "and you were dying right in front of me. I thought you were second on the list for a transplant. It was like…I thought that was it." His brow creased, as if he didn't understand what I was talking about. God, there were so many little details and I wanted to tell this story fast and dirty so I could get it over with.

"You hate your father already, so it's not like this is going to make it worse. I went to him because I wanted something."

"What did he want in exchange?" His voice was hard and cold, and the implications of his assumptions justified the tone.

"Forgiveness from you. Enough to get your mother back to him."

He put his hand over his face and rubbed his eyes. "That's what that whole thing was about. I barely remember it. I was in and out of consciousness ten times in a minute." He patted my hand, then rubbed my fingers. "What did you want?"

I balled my hand into a fist. I didn't want his affection. I couldn't bear to feel it stop when I put the pieces together for him.

"So, I saw Brad's list. I didn't understand how it worked. So I thought what I was seeing was...You were second, and I thought it meant you were going to die. It seemed like a guarantee. And Paulie Patalano was brain dead and right on the fourth floor."

Unable to stand the weight of his gaze, I looked in my lap, where his hand rested in mine, fourth finger still circled by the cheap silver keyring.

"I thought your father could get me access to Paulie's room."

He moved his hand away, placing it at his side. I wished he'd slapped me in the face. It would have been somehow kinder.

"Did he?"

"He did. He's very clever. And everything you said about him is probably right. But I was the one who went in there. I was going to do it. I was going to end him so you could get his heart." I didn't mention Jessica's part. What I'd done was my choice and my responsibility. Now wasn't the time to diffuse it with Jessica-shaped shadow play. "I knew what it meant. I knew that if my plan worked, you'd have a heart in your chest that you thought was stolen. You never would have felt right about yourself. I knew I was condemning you, in a way. And us. I knew you wouldn't forgive me. I was ending us. And I should say I'm sorry, but I'd do it again if I thought it would save your life."

"You didn't do it, though."

"Brad texted me while I was in the room. He had a heart from that poor guy in Ojai. The one who jogs and hates spicy food, apparently. So, I didn't have to go through with it."

He took my hand again and rubbed each finger as if considering their ability to do harm.

"God saved you," he whispered.

"You believe in God? You believe he'd step in and save me? And he'd kill someone to do it?"

"God was in Brad's text. I believe that. But swear to me, I mean I don't think that circumstance will recur, but swear to me you won't ever consider something like that again."

"I won't let you die if I can prevent it. I don't feel right about it. I won't pretend I do, but it's like how a soldier must feel when he kills the enemy. I'm sure it doesn't feel good, but there wasn't a choice. And if it comes to me not having a choice again, I'll do it again."

I searched his face for distaste, or foul rancor, and found none. Then I looked for disquiet or emotional blankness, and found none of that either. I couldn't read him, even when he took my arms and pulled me forward, onto him. I rested my head on his chest.

"I have to tell you," he said, "I'm scared of death. But you? You put death to shame."

"Do you still love me?"

"Yes."

"Are you going to leave me?"

"No."

"Do you forgive me?"

He took a long time to answer. I told myself it didn't matter, that his forgiveness was besides the point when I had his love.

"I fear you. I am in awe of you. I can't forgive you for something you didn't do."

I'd thought I was committed to him before. I thought I'd given him my whole heart, and that I owned him completely. But I hadn't. And maybe I'd spend the rest of his life realizing I'd never owned him, loved him or committed to him fully. Maybe it was a matter of the changing acoustics of an ever-expanding heart.

I kissed his scar, and he stroked my hair. I worked down his body, and took his cock in my mouth. I wanted to eat him alive, swallow his forgiveness, eat his compassion, to become him, to own his pain and kindness, his sadism and his maturity, holding it to myself, wrapped in a drum-tight skin of gratitude.

CHAPTER 9.

MONICA

I usually had a dream. I was in Sequoia, but it wasn't Sequoia. The hallways were narrower, the lights dimmer or blindingly bright—endlessly white and long. Doors everywhere, some locked some ajar. In my right hand beat a throbbing, pulsing heart, dropping blood onto the bleached linoleum. I didn't have long. I only had as much time as the blood in the heart, and I needed to get to Jonathan's room with it or he would die. Sometimes the hospital was empty, and I couldn't find the room. And sometimes it was populated with people who didn't know what the hell I was talking about or where I should go. Once, I dreamed the halls were lined with chicken coops, and Dr. Brad sent me in the wrong direction on purpose.

Jonathan always died. I always woke up in a state of grief and misery, and he was either next to me, or I was in an empty bed looking for a way to call him without worrying him.

The night after he reclaimed me in the studio, with every inch of my body stinging and alive, I expected to have that same dream. It would be as surprising and terrifying as it always was. But it didn't come. And not the night after, when he made me wait twelve minutes before touching me. Not over the next week as he broke me, pushed me, hurt me, until I was a puddle of emotional satisfaction. I never had that dream again, as if my subconscious was suddenly okay with the whole arrangement of my life, and my conscious brain was the only troublemaker.

He hurt me, but one thing he didn't do was bind me. When I asked him to, he spanked me for questioning him, but he still didn't tie me up.

I mistrusted this in quiet moments, but let it go. He was too good. The same man as he'd been. Still wise and kind, still generous and funny, but with an added helping of scorching cruelty in bed. He'd scared the dreams away, and I was safe at night, but in the day, I still carried my anxieties. Even when I forgot to worry, I reminded myself that I hated grey and pale pink, that copper and blood had the same smell, and that the heart machine in the hospital made the same beep as the timer in the coffee shop. My brain did its due diligence, creating panic as insurance against death.

Jonathan had been more productive. Six weeks after he returned from the hospital, he started forgetting his anti-rejection meds because of the complexities of dosing, and his immune system started slipping because he wasn't taking in enough nutrients. Then, soon after Valentine's Day, he found out I'd been staying home to watch him. He'd sliced the air with his hand and said, simply, "No."

He hired help.

Laurelin was a nurse which I normally wouldn't hold against her. But I wasn't normal. She came to the house to interview in the afternoon, after a long line of women and men who spoke to Jonathan about what he expected, what he needed and what they could do. They all smelled sanitized. I couldn't sit in the interviews, because the hospital stink caused me so much anxiety I wanted to throw up. I told Jonathan I had to practice, but I peeked in on every one, and every time he said one of them was no good, I felt relieved.

But Laurelin didn't smell like a hospital.
Nothing about her reminded me of Sequoia. Her
hair was the color of scrambled eggs, and her belly
was rounded with the beginnings of her first
trimester. She smiled a lot, which they all do, but
she seemed to be made of sunshine and she smelled
of rosewater.

I felt as if a blanket had been thrown over me
on a cold night, and I couldn't imagine she would
let anything happen to my husband.

"Her," I'd said. "You need to hire her."

"Really? Why is that?"

"She's pregnant. She's going to take good care
of you. I can feel it."

"What does taking care of me feel like?"

"It feels like the only right and good thing. And
she smells nice. And you like her, I can tell."

"I think she might be bossy."

"I'll take that as a yes."

So she was hired, and she'd been the bulwark
against my needling she was supposed to be. I could
travel and work without worrying, and without
Jonathan worrying that I was worrying. Maybe it
was a bad idea. Maybe Laurelin made our need to
communicate less urgent.

Four months after she was hired, and two weeks
after Jonathan reclaimed me, Laurelin shuffled in
wearing jeans and a sweatshirt even in the late June
warmth. She had the code for the front gate that
worked three mornings a week. She'd worked in the
infectious diseases unit of the Hollywood
Methodist, and couldn't continue while pregnant.

Jonathan had left his little blue book on the
counter for her. It was pliable leather with ruled
cream pages and a black ribbon marker. In it, he

kept notes about his diet, his exercise, and if he was late or early taking his rejection meds.

"Hi, Laurelin! How are you feeling?"

"Not bad." She pulled Jonathan's blue book and box of meds toward her. "I've skipped just about every complication I could." She put on a glitter face, swinging her blonde ponytail from one side to the other, then popped open the box of pills that had a day of the week and a time of day in each compartment.

"How much longer?"

"Seven weeks," she said, brows knotted about what she saw in Jonathan's little pill box. "What's this?" she asked.

"What's what?" I didn't look at her, just the teapot as I filled it.

She looked at her watch. "It's ten, and he hasn't taken his morning treatment."

I didn't say anything.

"Monica?"

"Yeah?"

"Where is he?" She flipped to the last page of the book.

"He's on a run."

She snapped the book closed definitively. "Well, we're going to have to have a little talk, the three of us."

I felt chastened. I shouldn't have. She worked for Jonathan, and thus, she worked for me, and it wasn't as if I was the one who had missed a handful of pills. That had been my husband, wanting just one more short tumble before his run, then breakfast, then his cubicle of meds.

Laurelin hummed and pulled the blender to her. She had packets of vitamin powders and access to the fridge so she set up his Shit Shake for that day and the two following.

I felt like I'd been let off the hook. I hadn't been able to resist him that morning. He wanted a tumble. No pain, no scene, no demands, just a one-two-three bite of vanilla cake. Delicious. Not something I wanted every day, but a good interlude between the usual screaming, bruising, games we played. I must have been smiling, because when I looked up, Laurelin was staring at me and smirking.

"I know you're still newlyweds—"

I slapped my hands over my ears. "La la la – stop it Laurelin!"

She ripped open a packet of powder and dumped it in the blender. "You can get on with it after he takes his meds."

"You know how responsible he is," I said.

"Generally."

"Can you not give him a hard time? I'll take care of it from now on."

She poured milk in the blender and shook it, peeking in the top. "You're away too often to keep that promise."

She was right. I knew when I was away, he was perfect, and when I was around he let things slip.

"Well, consider me chastened. I'm going to lunch, you can berate my husband when he gets back."

I kissed her on the cheek and ran out.

***

I spotted Darren halfway down the block from Terra Café. He looked taller by a few inches, possibly because Adam, who walked astride him, was only five eight. Darren keened a little to the left, bumping his boyfriend affectionately, and Adam nudged Darren with his elbow.

"You're late," I said.

"Oh, miss hotshot's on a schedule." Darren gave me jazz hands while Adam kissed my cheek.

"The line in this place is nuts. So this five minutes counts." I wagged my finger at him as if I meant it, which I didn't. Not even a little. I couldn't have cared less if he was late.

"Did you finish the EP?" Darren asked.

"Yesterday. It was great. I mean, all of it, every track I feel good about."

"How many?"

"Six."

"Nice." He looked up at the menu. Organic fair trade lunch, gourmet cakes and pies, vegan, free-range, grass-fed, gluten-free, cruelty-free, flavor-challenged, and the descriptions of what wasn't added, wasn't done, wasn't offered, took up half the board.

"You look different," Adam said, looking me up and down. He'd really grown on me with his sharp mouth and cutting sense of humor. If you could take a joke, he was the guy to hang around, and if you beat him to the punch, even better. Thin-skinned weeping willows need not apply.

"I'm the same."

"Just richer," Adam snapped back. Darren elbowed him and he laughed.

I shrugged. "There's that. But you're still buying your own lunch."

"But no," Adam continued. "Seriously, since the last time I saw you."

Darren cut in. "The last time you saw her she was in a hospital cafeteria. She hadn't eaten in weeks. It was a fucking nightmare."

They'd come to visit a few days after Jonathan had his transplant. I barely remembered it. No, I did remember it. It was Christmas. Darren had brought me a piece of holiday cake and I'd eaten it down to the last scrapings of frosting. The cake, I remembered, the conversation, which probably centered around physical damage and medical procedures, was lost.

We sat at a cramped spot by the window and put our number on the table. I'd seen Darren a lot since the hospital. He was the only one I'd told about the horrors of Sequoia Hospital. The recurrent dreams. The heart-gripping fear whenever I heard a machine beep, or saw an innocuous color combination. I told him how I went miles out of my way to avoid the hospital compound or any TV show with scenes in a medical facility. I even refused to use white sheets in the house, because the sheets in the hospital were white and I couldn't bear it.

He'd been there for me in the middle of the night when the next door alarm beeped and I freaked out, because it sounded like a heart monitor. He gave me directions when I got lost in West Hollywood because I couldn't find a way to get where I was going without going past Sequoia. He'd heard about all the dreams of the endless hospital hallways while Jonathan died in a room I couldn't find.

"When is he going back to work?" Adam asked. He traded real estate insurance products, so anything that happened in real estate was hugely interesting to me. I always had to make sure to only tell him things that had been announced publicly.

"He's selling most everything," I said.

"Really?" He considered his iced green tea latte. "He need more money?"

"Shut up." I flicked a few drops of condensation from my cup at him.

"Sorry."

"I mean, who wants to run an empire on borrowed time? At this point, it's either sell it all or go back to working like a dog. And that's all your getting out of me Mister Corporate Raider."

He rolled his eyes. "You going to tell her?" Adam asked Darren, biting the straw of his emerald-color latte.

"Tell me what?"

Darren pressed his fingers into his eyes as if he still had sleep in them.

"You are an unbelievable chickenshit," Adam mumbled.

"Fuck off."

"Okay," I held my hands up. "Listen, this is cute but if you guys haven't talked about this already I'd be happy to step outside while you—"

"Easy, it's not a big deal."

"Really?" Adam seemed put off.

"I'm moving out of Echo Park."

"You're moving in together!" I squealed joyfully. "That's awesome!"

"Yes, but that's not it. We did something impulsive, and we're just sticking with it," Darren said. "Before some asshole makes it illegal again."

I heard something about assholes at the end, but not really, because I'd scraped my chair back to come around the table. I plopped right in Darren's lap and hugged him. Adam got in on the action until we were a pile of happy limbs.

"Just say it so I know I'm not hugging you for buying a pot farm."

"We got married!" Adam said.

Three tables around us twisted around to look, then broke into applause. I stood up and clapped some more, and Adam pushed his lips into Darren's cheek. My ex-boyfriend blushed.

I sat when the applause died and the food arrived.

"So," I said, "why now? Or then? Or when?"

"Yesterday," Darren answered. "The deal was, when I had a foothold as a musician—"

Adam interrupted between taps on his phone, "And I was not holding my breath—"

"Oh, fuck you."

"It's got nothing to do with your talent and you know that, honey."

"Whatever. That was the deal. I've been working at Redlight Studios pretty regularly, and Harry and I have been working on some really broad, commercial stuff."

"Yeah," I said. "I know all this. Why are you stalling?"

"I don't want you to compare this to what you get, because you, I mean you're getting a different kind of deal."

"Oh. My. God. You got signed."

"It's nothing. It's music for a video game. *City of Dis*, if you've heard of it."

"I have."

"Well, it's a good gig, and good money. And I didn't even mention it because who cares? But it just got us noticed enough that we're getting signed by Beowolf Records for a really small thing—"

Adam dropped his phone onto the table, "And this is why I said, 'marry me now, or I'm done with you,' because nothing is a big enough deal for him.

He'd accept my proposal after his fifth Grammy, maybe."

"Are you guys having a party or something? I want to give gifts and get drunk. You owe me that."

"When we get a place," Adam said. "And not in the slums of Los Angeles, so sorry. Something nice on the west side with a big enough yard for a reception."

The look on Darren's face told met here had been some contention over either the size or the location, but I said nothing. I'd get it out of him later.

My phone rang.

"Let me get this," I slid the phone off the table and walked outside.

Jonathan and I had a new deal. Any time, any place, if he called I picked up. If he called during a show, I had to pick up in front of the audience. The only way to avoid that was to tell him when I was going to be on stage, when I was going to be in the studio, and he'd only call if it was an emergency.

"Hello Goddess," he said.

"Hi." I felt warm and giddy.

"I think we should cancel on Sheila tomorrow."

"Why?"

"I noticed you were walking straight. Can't have that."

As appealing as the thought of him making it hard for me to walk was, he needed to be at Sheila's tomorrow.

"We can work around it."

"Since when are you so eager to see my family?"

The rule of never lying to save each other pain was still in effect. I couldn't travel thinking he wanted me gone, and he couldn't chase me out to save me from being around him. We were to be direct in our insecurities and our desires, even if they were going to hurt.

"I want to go," I said, telling the truth but keeping a tiny lie to myself. "That's the fact. I happen to love almost all of your sisters as much as Margie."

"Truth?"

"Truth."

"Come home."

"May I finish lunch?"

"Hurry. I want to fuck you blind."

Fluid rushed between my legs. I almost buckled at the knees.

We hung up and I dialed Margie while leaning against a parking meter.

"Yes?" she snapped.

"He's trying to wiggle out of tomorrow."

"You have one job, Monica. One job."

"I can do my best but—"

"For the tenth time. He is not going to have a heart attack when we yell 'surprise.' You're going to give yourself an ulcer."

"The doctor said no stress. That's stressful."

"Is he taking all his rejection meds?"

"Yes."

"Eating right?"

"Yes."

"Is he exercising?"

I sighed, frustrated. She was building a case and the jury would find in her favor. "Jogs miles and miles a day."

"Is there any way possible that he is not taking care of himself?"

"He's a model citizen."

"So, what's the problem?"

"I love him and I don't want to lose him. That's the problem. When are you going to tell him about the Swiss thing?"

"Tomorrow I'm going over there to get some things signed. I'll bring it up then."

"Okay." What I said with that "okay" was that she'd better do it or I was going to blurt something out in the bedroom. We'd agreed that it should be presented as business, and Margie was business, but one more day and it was going to feel like withholding.

"What did you get him for his birthday?" Margie changed the subject.

"I wrote him a song."

Her sigh was audible over the traffic. "You're a good wife. It's almost sickening."

CHAPTER 10.

MONICA

The morning of Jonathan's birthday, I woke him up by putting his cock in my mouth, and he twisted me around and put his mouth on me at the same time. He didn't even say good morning before I came in his mouth, groaning with his dick down my throat.

"Monica, you didn't ask."

"But, wait. We're in scene?"

"Get up and stand by the window."

I had to write his song, and dinner was at five. I was already cutting it close. I wasn't a particularly quick songwriter. Since we'd both collapsed without fucking the night before, this could go on for hours.

But I couldn't hesitate. I wasn't afraid he'd beat me harder. I was afraid he'd think I didn't want to. So I stood up and faced the back patio, already naked. I wanted to do this, do it hard, and write the song, because I had no idea what I wanted to make of it. I had no idea what to say except everything.

"Put your hands on the glass."

I leaned forward and put my fingertips to the back doors. Behind me, I heard his belt buckle clink and his fly zip as he put his pants on.

"Whole hand. Come on, Monica. Commit." He spanked my ass playfully. I put my whole palm on the glass and stretched my back. "Open those legs."

I did it, and he pressed on my lower back until my ass was all the way up.

"Good."

"Thank you."

He nonchalantly went out the back door and looked out over the ocean. The salt breeze blew his hair back. Then, as if noticing something for the first time, he played his fingers on the bamboo stalks in the patio's stone planter as if they were strings on a harp. They were green and over two feet long, growing tight as a porous boundary between us and the beach... and there was no way he just happened to notice them today. My king wasn't that impulsive. He yanked one of the shoots out and snapped out his pocketknife, which also just happened to be in his jeans. He cut the roots off the stalk and shortened it on the pointy end, right in front of me.

He walked back in the house with it.

"Now," he said from behind me. "I think we've talked about your orgasms before, and who owns them."

"You do." I looked out the window. Without him there, I felt exposed, breasts hanging, ass up.

"No one can see you, Monica." He slapped my ass.

"Yes, sir."

"Do you believe me?"

"I want to."

He swatted me with the bamboo, lightly, as if testing. Then he did it harder. It was no thicker than a pinky, and that second time, it made a whipping sound before it landed with a *crack*.

Then he did it a little harder.

I sucked in my breath.

"How is that?" he asked.

"Good, sir."

He cracked it again, at the topmost fleshy part of my ass. The sting was incredible, searing me. I felt like my flesh was opening. Then he did it again, an inch or so below the last stroke. I let out an *mmm* sound, biting my lips together. And he did it again, and there was a rhythm to it, a slow build as he worked his way down to my knees, searing pain leaving blossoming pleasure in its wake. Two taps to aim, one to awaken the skin, and one to make me scream in pain, and it went *thwap thwap* thwap THWAP. *thwap thwap* thwap THWAP. *thwap thwap* thwap THWAP.

***

In the little studio in the guest house, the piano keys went *tap tap* tap TAP. *tap tap* tap TAP, as I searched for the notes. I shifted in my seat. Jonathan had given my ass and thighs plenty of aftercare, but I wouldn't be comfortable for a couple of days. I'd think of him and his mastery of me whenever I sat or walked, which was the point.

I was slow, and I had only a few hours. Slow with words and clunky with melody. I missed Gabby. She made things work in minutes. I did a poem to the snap of my fingers and she would sit there, tap out the rhythm, and embellish it until we had a song. Not every song was good, but at least I knew what I was dealing with before ten minutes had passed.

But me, by myself, I had a hard time. I think the work was good, in the end, but I wasn't producing well under pressure, because I didn't even know what the song was about, except time.

Ten years. It had been impossible to talk about that length of time without impaling myself on it. It was so far off, and tomorrow. It was a lie, because it could be so much more if he took care of himself and played by the rules. Even after his heart gave out, if the doctors saw he ate right and took his medicine, he'd get another heart if it came available. It had been done. And was it really ten? Because there was a very healthy guy in Wyoming who had his for a record breaking twenty-five years and there were new advances in anti-rejection meds every day and and and....

None of this was going to matter if he was dead. So, I'd planned for the eventuality by girding myself, day after day. It was going to hurt. I was going to be in the hospital again, crying over him, alone, vulnerable, and scared. As it was, a shaft of ice stabbed my spine whenever I passed Sequoia Hospital, and the knowledge that one day, soon, I was going back for the same reason froze me in panic.

All I did was pray for him. The first six months of our marriage had been one big prayer without end, amen.

I couldn't get control of it by running or staying, and he wanted children. Children. I'd lost my father and it crushed me. He'd wanted to have children and disappear when the oldest was nine. Or eight. Or who even knew. With a hopeless mother who had lost the love of her life. No amount of money was going to cure that.

And now, six months later, with his breath in my ear and his sexual dominance reestablished, was anything solved? No. Nothing was. But God damn if I was going to sing him a birthday song about a house because it was the only thing we could agree on.

He was better than that.

We were better than that.

I had a few hours to write him a new song. Not about how much time we had. Not about all our failings, but about what we meant to each other. But about how fulfilling and worthwhile those ten years could be, if I stopped squinting to the distance for the end of them.

coda.

Tap tap tap TAP. *tap tap* tap TAP.

CHAPTER 11.

JONATHAN

Jogging. Herbal tea. Rabbit food. Jesus Christ, how had I survived six months without making my wife beg for mercy? I stood in the driveway looking at our house from the street for the hundredth time. It was deep in and behind a wall of roses, but who could see? From what angle? If I fucked her on the back patio, were her shaking tits visible from the public part of the beach? Could they hear her scream next door?

The low-slung mid-century glass box was so well-designed and so well-placed that unless we kept the lights on at night and fucked against the window in a certain part of the room, we couldn't be seen. I knew that from the second day. But it *felt* like we were exposed, and she liked that. That morning, before she'd gone to lunch I'd taken her against that window. Her handprints were still on it, like two frosted starfish. She'd put her hands against the glass when I told her to, ass out, legs spread almost, but not quite wide enough. I stuck my fingers in her. She was soaked, and I hadn't even started. Was it my commands? Or the window?

"No one can see you, Monica." I'd said, then slapped her ass.

"Yes, sir."

"Do you believe me?"

"I want to."

I caned her hard and thoroughly until my arm ached and she was a groaning mess. It was her way of telling me she trusted me, but needed that shade of doubt. It brought her so close to orgasm I barely had to touch her with my dick before she came.

I might even learn to like this house.

"What are you doing in the middle of the street?" came a voice from behind me. I didn't turn around. I knew my sister's voice better than I knew my own mother's.

"You should call before you show up," I said. Margie was hanging half out the window of her Mercedes. Waving her arm for me to get out of the way of the driveway. "I'm a newlywed, you know."

"We had an appointment." She pulled in and I followed on foot, letting the gate close behind me.

I opened the door for her when she stopped. "We did." I said. "I forgot."

She got out, yanking her briefcase free of the passenger seat floor. "You shouldn't have fired your assistant before you were finished with your business."

"I'm sick of calendars and commitments."

She made a thick sound in her throat that could have been interpreted as a *harrumph*, except that was too passive-aggressive for my sister. If she had something to say, she never let a vocal tic replace a well-placed barb.

I led her inside.

"You want something?" I asked, opening the fridge.

"Nice place," she said, putting her briefcase on the island bar. "I almost went to the old one. Up in the hills." She snapped it open.

I got her a glass of water with no ice. She thanked me as if she'd actually asked for it. But she didn't have to. I knew her at least that well. I opened a bottle of water for myself. I was off Perrier. Carbonation was on the No Intake list.

"Is it what you expected?" I asked. She had been the sister I leaned on most. I never talked abut my emotional life before the surgery, but I had to,

71

or I'd break. Margie had been my valve, because she was honest and straight, and she knew when to shut the hell up.

"I expected a house cut in half with masking tape," she answered, taking papers out and laying them in neat piles on the granite.

"Did I make it sound that bad?"

"For two people suffering from Post-Traumatic Stress? I think you're doing great. Not that I have anything healthy to compare you to." She clicked a pen and handed it to me. "Sign where I put yellow tabs. Initial on the purple."

I started from left to right, signing away about ten years of my life. The business I rebuilt for Dad in repayment for silence over Rachel. Twenty-two to thirty-two – over a billion and a quarter in assets in a managed trust. He could have it. Sale of the hotels, except K, where I met Monica. I wasn't ready to let that go. Another half a billion in real estate to a trust Margie would manage and share. My responsibility would be to do nothing but take care of myself.

"You think you might get bored?" Margie asked when I was halfway through the stacks.

"Yes. But I don't know what to do about it."

"There's this thing I heard about. You might be interested. Could kill some time. Definitely burn through some cash."

"Go on."

"In Switzerland. They're really close on an artificial heart."

"No."

"It's made from tissue. It doesn't need an external battery."

"No."

"They need a lot of money for development, but you have it."

"Am I speaking the wrong language? No."

"Why?"

"I don't like the Swiss. The cheese offends me."

"Nice answer. Got a reason that makes sense?"

I put the pen down. I knew my mouth was set because I felt the tension in my jaw.

"What would be the point?" I said. "To get my wife's hopes up so that it won't work? So I die anyway? The sooner she starts coping with it, the better."

She pushed the pen toward me. "Finish up."

I got back to signing at the tabs. Full signature for yellow. Initials at purple. "I have the Arts Foundation to run. That'll keep me busy."

"Yeah. And you don't have to waste your time hoping for anything. You don't have to build a future."

"I'm the one who wants kids."

"That's not a future if you're dead. That's called a legacy."

I dotted the last i and crossed the last t, flopping the contract closed. "Just like a lawyer to get hung up on semantics."

"Just like a man." She restacked her papers, clacking them against the counter. "You just want to piss on the world one last time like it's a fire hydrant you'll never see again. I don't blame her for holding out on you."

Coming from anyone else, I would have been enraged. But Margie's love was so unconditional, I didn't know if she could ever say anything to make me truly angry.

"You know this is not about legacy."

"Not consciously."

73

"It's about Monica."

"The everlasting gift of your DNA? Way to woo a girl."

I laughed. I had nothing else for her. I couldn't even explain myself to myself.

"It's nice to see you laugh, little brother. I thought they'd transplanted your sense of humor there for awhile."

"Are you staying for lunch? I could stand to be insulted for another hour."

"Sorry." She plopped her papers in her briefcase. "Some of us have to work."

"I have a thing," I said, walking her to the door. "For the birthday dinner tomorrow. I need you and Sheila to help."

She raised an eyebrow at me while she snapped the case closed.

"A thing?"

"You'll like it. It involves jewelry."

"I hate jewelry."

"You'll like this."

CHAPTER 12.

MONICA

I exited the studio in the mid afternoon completely unsatisfied with my work. I went into the kitchen and, seeing as Jonathan wasn't around, reached for his box of pills.

I don't know where I got into the habit of thinking it was all right to count someone's meds. From living with Gabby, maybe. Jonathan had Laurelin to monitor him, make sure his medication was taken, and help him mind his P's and Q's. That didn't stop me from peeking in his little plastic box with the days of the week on it.

Too many sets and subsets of pills. No wonder he needed a medical professional.

"Stop it," I told myself, snapping the box shut. I pushed it back into the corner between the toaster and the fridge. But it was too late. The medicines had a smell, and they brought it all back. The inevitable images of him dying in that fucking hospital, his heart breaking right out of his chest. The colors of the hospital lounge carpet, the paint, the cafeteria, the recovery room, all of it flashed before me. I closed my eyes as if that would drown out the smells and colors of those weeks.

"He's fine," I said to myself. "Stop it."

"Stop what?"

Jonathan came in from the patio, slick with sweat and ocean water. He'd been jogging.

"Stop tracking sand all over the floor. Look at this mess!"

"Why?" He grabbed me by the waist and pulled me into him. "Afraid it'll scratch your back?" He pushed me into the kitchen island and bit my neck at the curve.

"Don't leave a mark!" I pushed him away, not that it did anything. "We're going to Sheila's and—"

I couldn't finish when he stuck his hand between my legs and yanked my pants down by the crotch.

"We just did it," I groaned. I could have ended the California drought with what flowed between my legs.

"Define 'just.'" He unceremoniously pulled my shirt up and grabbed a nipple. My body went on high alert.

"I'm still sore."

"That's how I like you."

I pushed him away for real. "I don't want to use my safe word for stupid bullshit, Drazen. But back off. I'm making a snack. What do you want?"

He smiled, taking the hint but not believing it. "You, with butter and jelly."

"I have a baguette left from last night."

"Fine." He pulled my shirt down.

"You should have protein. An egg or something."

"There's enough protein in my morning shake to create an entire mammalian species."

I kissed him gently. "You should try the bread with the chimichuri."

"Hell, no." He opened the fridge and leaned into where the condiments hung out. His running pants hung low on his hips.

"I see you looking at me," he said, still rooting around the back.

"You gained weight."

"These are my fat pants." He smiled, shutting the door and putting the goods on the counter. I unscrewed the cap on the hot sauce and ripped off a piece of baguette.

"Try," I said, dipping the bread into the sauce. I got as little as possible, because I wanted my husband to get over the spicy food thing. I knew it embarrassed him.

I held it up for him. "Come on," I said. "I made this with my own hands, with my mother. Think of the generations of women that have perfected it for the sake of this one moment in time."

"Not to be dramatic."

"I'll get a samba band in here if you like. *Cha cha chadda.*" I swung my hips to the rhythm, with my piece of bread out. He grabbed my wrist and held it still. I froze. Had I insulted his masculinity or something?

He locked eyes with me, then tore them away, kissing the inside of my arm, my wrist, and taking the bread in his mouth. He chewed. I waited. He had zero change of expression, and I smiled a little.

He swallowed. "I feel like my face is burning from the inside."

"Well, you look gorgeous."

He let my hand go and screwed the top back on the chimichuri.

"You're just seeing a free man," he said.

"Oh, right, Margie came today. Did you get rid of everything?"

"I gave up every hotel from A to J. I kept the one where I met you. I'm sentimental like that."

"Did she tell you about the Swiss thing?"

He froze. I swallowed. Was this more complicated than I thought? Was it too expensive an investment?

"Yes," he said.

"And?"

"I'll think about it."

"Really?"

"I—"

I had an explosion I couldn't control or foresee, where all my pent up feelings went off like controlled detonation, except the building didn't collapse, but took off like a rocket. I spread my arms and threw them around his neck, wrapping my around his waist. He was thrown back a step catching me.

"Jesus, Monica."

"Happy birthday, baby." I kissed him seven times. I couldn't stop, but then I had to talk. "They're so close they just need a push. I know it's a lot of money but it's worth it when they figure out the rejection thing it needs its own special rejection meds which they're also developing and then a healthy test subject who is—"

"Whoa whoa."

"—young, with no secondary problems."

"Monica."

"It's you. You. Especially if you fund it they have to make it you. And it lasts forever. You'll have to get hit by a bus when you're a hundred and ten."

He loosened his grip until my feet hit the floor. "Do you know what the odds are of it working?" he said when I let him go.

"Great!" I stuffed the bread back into the bag. "The odds are great. I mean, I don't know. I didn't ask. But the odds of the one you have lasting even twenty years are worse, since they're like, zero."

I felt like a giddy schoolgirl. I wanted to sing and dance and the smile on my face was totally involuntary. I could barely contain myself. I felt as if the past seven months might be erased; put away in some jar in the china cabinet where we could ogle how cute and silly it all had been.

Jonathan leaned against the counter, clicking the ice in his water glass, staring into it as if it were a problem. I felt crazy and childish in comparison. I cleared my throat, choking back the relief, trying to find that worry again. But it wouldn't go away. I was over the moon and he was still on the earth.

I breathed deeply, trying to calm down. I was overreacting for sure, but it was his heart, his life, his chest, and if he was somber over it, then I could take it down a notch.

I moved the bread bag three inches. Touched a pan, shifting it on the stove. Smiled as I turned a knickknack a quarter way around. My mother had given it to me. It said BELIZE.

"I thought you were going to eat something," Jonathan said.

"Fuck it." I got in front of him. "I want you for snack."

I dropped to my knees and yanked his sweatpants down.

"Okay, Monica—"

I gave him big eyes from below. "You don't want me to suck your cock?" I felt him harden in my hand.

"I'd love a blowjob, thank you. I have to take a handful of pills. Then I'm going to shower. So I need you to go upstairs. Take your clothes off and be ready for a quick go before we leave. And when I say ready, I mean, mouth open, hands behind your back."

"Yes, sir," I said through a smile.

"Your legs should be open all the way this time. I mean it. We're on a tight clock."

"Yes."

"Have I mentioned how much I love being married to you?"

"Not today."
"Let me finish up here and I'll show you."

CHAPTER 13.

JONATHAN

I loved being married to Monica, at least, once we reestablished full participation by both parties. The weeks following my visit to the studio, minus the constant medication, had been exactly what I'd wanted from the honeymoon we never had.

Things would get back to normal soon, whatever that was. I still couldn't find a taste for the food I used to like. Anything spicy tasted like poison, and I craved sour foods as if I was pregnant. I thought less and less about having a strange piece of meat inside me, my chest didn't feel as heavy with attention, as often. I was in a routine with Laurelin, the medicine, the nutrition, and my odd addiction to jogging which made the team of doctors happy.

Otherwise. Normal. For somebody.

But at least I could still make plans for Monica's body and execute them. At least, if I couldn't eat the spicy chimichuri, which we apparently had a never-ending supply of, I could spoon feed her while she was on her hands and knees.

I'd overheard her fielding calls from the people she worked with, putting them off, apologizing. She was an artist and she'd need to get back to it soon. We still hadn't talked about how to manage that part of our lives, because I had to admit for the first time that I didn't want her to travel so much, but I didn't know what to do about it. The visions of my heart leaving my body persisted. Sometimes it flopped around the floor, squirting blood, sometimes it only came halfway out, and sometimes when I scratched the itchy scar, my fingers went through the soft tissue and touched the foreign, beating thing, and in response it detached itself and slid into my palm.

And Monica was always there in these waking dreams. In the easiest ones, she was simply horrified. In the worst of them, I was driving and killed her when I died at the wheel. But travelling? I was convinced the heart would stay on the ground when I flew, as if tethered not to my body, but to the state of California. I'd ruin her trip and probably her life. I was never scared of my own death. I'd dealt with that already, but it's effect on Monica would be shattering.

None of it was rational. None of it made sense. And my nearly physical ache for children made the least sense of all the crazy nonsense I believed. Knowing that didn't shake the fear or the longing away.

I'd managed to wiggle out of travelling, until we drove down to Sheila's place in Palos Verdes. The June evening left the sky palette-knifed in orange and navy, and the temperature hung between inoffensively cold, and completely generic. With the top down and Monica next to me in the Jag, twisted in the seat, the weather was perfect.

"Are you going to sit like that in front of my sisters?"

"Hey, if you wanted me to sit straight you should have been a little gentler."

"You didn't marry me for my gentle ways."

She poked me in the ribs and I laughed, but she sat straighter.

"Is there any country in the world you haven't been to?" she asked.

"Probably."

"Any one you want to go to?"

"Iceland. But I'm not cleared yet."

"Yes you are. You haven't asked Dr. Solis at all. We could send a bunch of shit shakes ahead, and make sure whatever cardiac unit there was knew you were coming."

I didn't answer right away. We were communicating, but that didn't mean I should answer rashly. I pulled off the 110, slowing my car, and my thoughts.

"The thought of it," I said. "It's…" I drifted off. I knew what the honest answer was, but it was hard to speak aloud.

"We can do everything to make it less scary—"

"I didn't say I was scared."

"Well, I am." She reached over and took my hand, looking out her side of the car. "Anyway. The food's really bland there. You should like it."

I reached under her arm and tickled her. She squealed and twisted away.

What was I going to do with her? Besides spank her raw and love her senseless? At some point, I was going to keep our honesty promise and break it to her that even if I funded the artificial heart, I wasn't going to test it. But her relief and happiness were too precious and delicate. I hoped some other obstacle would present itself in the meantime. Blood type, body size, anything.

I went through the gate and parked in front of Sheila's house, pulling the emergency brake.

"About the Swiss thing," I said.

"Yeah?"

"If it's not what you think or if it's not going to work out, you're going to be disappointed."

"It'll work out. I know it."

She didn't wait for me to come around. She just opened the door and got out, bouncing as if it was someone's birthday.

CHAPTER 14.

MONICA

Jonathan followed behind, flipping his keys in his palm, spinning them around a finger, flipping again. Spin. Flip. Spin. Flip. All in the rhythm of his gait, like a perfectly tuned instrument of movement and sound. He wore a white shirt open at the collar, sleeves rolled to the elbow, and jeans that fit as if custom built for him. Jogging miles every morning had toned his legs and added grace to his gait.

I rang Sheila's bell. The door was wide enough to fit two adults walking abreast, so I didn't know how he was supposed to get in without seeing everyone. But it hadn't been my job to hide everyone. It had been my job to get him there on time.

He slipped his hand across the bare skin of my shoulder and grasped me by the back of the neck, saying nothing and owning me completely. I relaxed right into the warmth of his hand.

The door opened. Sheila wore a pair of skinny jeans and a lavender hoodie. Bare feet. Hair brushed for a change.

"Happy Birthday!" she said.

"Thanks." He reached out and kissed her on the cheek, leaving his other hand on me as if I'd run away.

Was the party off? Had something happened? Where was the big opening salvo? Sheila got out of the way. Jonathan guided me in the door, and I greeted her. Looking over her shoulder, I caught sight of the buffet, and felt more than saw the presence of other people.

It wasn't until Jonathan stepped in and the door closed behind him that the shout of "Surprise!"

came all at once, at incredible volume, from an impossible number of people who appeared from the hall, behind the couch, the patio, as if a switch had been flicked.

Jonathan stood in the doorway a second, then clutched his chest and took a step back. Mouth open, eyes wide, as if in shock and surprise at the pain.

I went blind, reaching for him, everything shut out but the sounds of the beeping machines, the stench of alcohol, the shadowed lines of the blinds falling across his white face in the afternoon.

Hands on me. Strong arms, and the sounds of the room pierced the veil of terror.

Laughter.

A few dozen people laughing hysterically, and a collective *awwww.*

Jonathan held me up, looking down at me with a smile.

"You asshole!" I said.

"Come on," he said. "It was funny."

"No, it wasn't," I whispered softly so he'd know I was serious. I dropped my register and changed my inflection to sound like him when he didn't want an argument. "Don't ever do that to me again."

"I think it was that bite of chimichuri." He rubbed his stomach and smiled.

I didn't laugh. Didn't smile. Didn't give him anything but ice cold anger. He paused, looking pensively at me, pressing his lips together before he said, "I'm sorry."

I was still shaken. I couldn't forgive him. Not yet, and luckily I didn't have to, because Leanne put a drink in my hand.

"Thanks," I said.

"He's a fucker." For a fashion designer, she usually dressed in clothes that were no more exciting then the average plain Jane, and well, to be honest she was kind of a slob. But that day, her jeans were rippling with shades of blue and her hands were covered in deep indigo in the creases.

I swished the drink. It was a yellow, juicy thing with ice. Behind me, Jonathan gladhanded and laughed.

"What happened to your hands?" I asked.

"We're doing denim tie-dye in India." She indicated her jeans, which went from deepest indigo to pale sky in irregular patterns.

"Hm," was all I said.

"Not perfected yet, obviously. And it's messing with the sideseams." She grabbed her beltloops and yanked her pants up.

"God, I wish you'd brush your hair," Margie said to Leanne from behind me.

Leanne's bracelets bangled when she extended her silver-ringed middle finger at her sister. They tormented each other for a few more seconds, Drazen-style, and I twisted around to look for Jonathan. I found him chatting with Eddie and another guy, perfectly happy, no chest pain, arms gesturing without stiffness. He wasn't having a heart attack.

As if summoned by my attention, he looked at me through the crowd and winked.

Asshole.

Gorgeous asshole.

I excused myself and went to the kitchen. Staff buzzed around, slapping the oven open and shut, talking the language of waitstaff I knew all too well. Eileen Drazen stood by the sink in sensible tan pants and jacket, throwing her head back as if she'd just taken a pill. She sipped whiskey and turned around.

"Hey," I said. "How are you doing?"

I reached in the cabinet for a glass. She and I had met under terrible circumstances, and once I understood that, and she understood that I wasn't after her son's money, she was still made of ice. But at least she was only cold, rather than cold and dismissive.

"Fine. You?"

"I'm getting over the psychotic break I nearly had a few minutes ago." I filled the glass from the fridge door.

"Yes. On the scale of inappropriate jokes, that was deep in the red. You should make him suffer for it."

"Where's Declan?" I asked. I wanted to avoid him. He'd laughed off the three-doctors incident as simple misinformation, and I didn't have a fact to hold against him. So, like the rest of his children, I simply didn't trust him.

"Around." She waved her ring-thick hand. "Everyone is here, somewhere. I lose count of all of them."

"Have you seen Leanne's jeans?"

I said it to get a reaction and she shuddered as if it was scandalous. My mother in law was such a backwards prude that sometimes I wondered if it was all an act to protect a burning sexuality.

"I think it's cute," I said, sipping my water.

"You would," she said without reproach. "I've learned to stop concerning myself with my children's tastes. They get away and then, poof, they're not your responsibility. They're just people who invite you over for holidays."

I nodded.

"How many does he want?" Eileen asked.

"Ten or more," I said, putting my empty glass in the sink.

Eileen barked a little laugh. "Men."

"Yeah."

"They figure if they have the money for a staff they can breed to their heart's content."

"You didn't want eight kids?"

"I wanted seven. Though the eighth?" She shrugged with a smile. "He'll do. It was nice to have a boy. Broke up the catfights over who used the last of the conditioner."

I laughed. "Really? With all your staff? You ran out of conditioner?"

"Your husband was pouring it down the sink. The joker. No matter how much Delilah bought he dumped it or hid it."

I caught sight of Eddie in a tan suit and red tie.

"Ed," Eileen said. "Nice to see you." The double kissed.

"You too, Mrs. Drazen."

I rarely saw Eddie Milpas in his social setting, where he knew Jonathan from college. Typically, he was the guy in the engineering room who made everyone else nervous. So I nearly burst out laughing when he called Eileen Mrs. Drazen.

"Come to check on the catering?" Eileen asked.

"Came to steal away this lady," he replied, cocking his head toward me.

"Do we have to talk about business?" I asked.

"If you'd call me back—"

"My cue to leave." Eileen said, and without another word, she was gone, leaving me with Eddie and the constantly moving catering staff.

"I'm sorry," I said. "I was going to call you on Monday."

"Which Monday, exactly?"

"This coming—"

"Look, I know you have other things on your mind. So I'm not going to sit here and watch you fidget."

I crossed my arms. "I'm not fidgeting."

"Can I give you a piece of friendly advice?"

"No."

"Professional advice then. One hundred percent free. Get yourself an agent to filter your damn calls."

I laughed softly at the irony. That was exactly what I'd been trying to do when I met Jonathan.

Eddie continued, "If I wasn't friends with your boyfriend—"

"Husband."

"You'd miss out on the opportunity of a lifetime if I didn't happen to be at this party."

"Okay, you've got my attention."

"Your EP is releasing in a few weeks. Right about then, Quentin Marshall is doing a charity song with everyone."

"Everyone?"

"Everyone. It's like those Christmas songs for Ethiopia, but for the bushmen in Australia or some shit. Omar. Brad Frasier. The Glocks. Benita. The list will knock you over. They have a space for a girl act like you, but here's the thing."

My heart pounded. This did sound like something groundbreaking for my career. A small fry like me, associated with big names like that could get my name out to people who had never heard me before. It could give me credibility and standing. And if it was a little after the EP was out, even better.

"Okay," I said. "Tell me the thing."

"They have to herd all these cats, and that means it could record on a dime any time between the fifteenth and the thirtieth, and the big names? Well, they call the shots. They get there when they get there. The less established artists have to be ready to go."

"I'm ready."

"Can you fly to New York tomorrow?"

"Tomorrow? New York?"

"Quentin Marshall? Hello?"

My throat had gone dry. I wanted to go. I wanted to get on a plane immediately and sit in the studio waiting for The Glocks to show up. I wanted to hear Omar sing in a studio. I could learn so much from that guy. He had a sound no one else could emulate. If I could watch him, I was sure I could pick up some tips.

"I don't know," I said.

"You don't know?"

"I have to ask Jonathan."

He put his hands up. "Fine. You have until tomorrow."

"Tomorrow is Sunday."

"Music doesn't take the weekend off."

"Okay. I'll call you by tomorrow night."

"Noon. That's the best you get. I have a line of people who would scratch your eyes out for this opportunity."

"Monica," Margie said, poking her head in. "We need you at the piano."

I scuttled out.

I glanced at the counter before following Margie. The catering staff hovered over a cake, lighting thirty-three candles. It seemed like enough fire to burn the house down, but that was the point.

A man who almost died at thirty-two deserved every single flame.

Stop.

I needed to stop obsessing over the transplant. I hadn't thought that until his birthday. Up until then, I'd given my worry a wide berth, as if it was insurance against something bad happening, but I'd let healthy concern metastasize into a cancer, and I was perfectly happy with it taking over my life until I dreaded singing Happy Birthday, because it sounded like a dirge.

I knew where the piano was from my last visit, when Sheila had insisted I play. I'd thought she was trotting me out like a trained monkey, which I resented for a few seconds, but once my fingers hit the keys, I realized what she'd done. I played *Wade In the Water* for his family, and music did what music does, it brought us together and gave us something to talk about. It was a way into our shared humanity. I loved music before I loved my husband, and it would outlast the two of us. As I stroked out a scale in the parlor with thirty people in attendance, I let myself love it again.

I caught Jonathan's eye across the room. He was fingering an apple with his nephew David. I knew the positioning. Split-fingered fastball, and David, at ten, was too young for it. I shook my head at Jonathan and took my hand from the keys long enough to wave my finger "no no" at him. He smiled, winked, and showed David the whipping motion that would get the ball to split, along with his nephew's young tendons.

He's not teaching our kids that.

"Uptempo, people!" I cried just as the cake appeared.

91

Happy Birthday—well, there's not much you can do with it when everyone's singing and not listening to the piano. I smiled. Fuck it. I gleefully let everyone else set the tempo and sang along in the dragged out rhythm. No one knew why I was smiling. Not even Jonathan, who came up and leaned on the piano.

Sheila brought the blazing white confection, placing it on top of the piano as we sang, "*yoooooooouuuu!*"

His face lit golden, his smile a true thing, from his beautiful candlelit green eyes to his borrowed heart, he blew out his candles. Or tried. No one could blow out thirty three candles (and one for good luck) in one breath.

"Nice effort," I said, standing. He put his arm around me and we blew together. I clapped and faced him. I wanted a kiss, but he glanced down at the cake, then at me, then back at the cake, then at me, as if he was trying to tell me something.

I looked down at it, thinking we'd missed a candle.

And we had. One little bugger was still bopping along, but I didn't blow it, because inside the ring of candles sat an open, frosting-caked velvet box, and inside the was a ring.

"Jonathan?"

He plucked the candle out of the cake.

"That was the candle I hold for you." He blew it, and the flame popped up again.

Thirty people and ten kids said "*Awwww.*"

He pursed his lips in a smile. "I didn't know there were going to be so many people here," he said quietly. Margie took the candle from his fingers. It still burned. It must have been one of those parlor trick candles, and it was sweet.

"What are you doing?" I asked, still confused. He guided me back onto the piano stool. I sat. "We're already married."

"Not properly," he said, picking the ring out of the box. "Not on my own power and not for the right reasons."

Were there dozens of people in the room? I couldn't hear them. I couldn't see them. Only this man, this king, getting on his knee in front of me.

"Jonathan, you don't have to, I…"

"You going to give me your hand or not?"

"I can't." I put them in the corners of my eyes as if to press the tears away. "I'm using them. Hang on."

"Get on with it!" a male voice called from the crowd.

"Shut the fuck up, Pat!" someone else said.

Jonathan touched my left wrist, and I brought my hand down. I didn't wear the borrowed diamond any more. Just the keyring wedding band.

"Will you marry me, Monica?"

I sniffed back a bunch of cry, and before I could answer, he continued, looking up at me. "Will you have a normal engagement with me? Will you get to know me on any given Tuesday?" He shook his head quickly, as if making it all up on the spot and discarding an idea. "Can we plan a real wedding and argue over seating arrangements? Can we find the things we agree on naturally? Flowers. Invitations. Whatever is important to *us*. I want us to be right with the world. I want us to take our time, because you're worth it. We are worth it. Nothing skimped or rushed. You deserve all of it. Everything."

Doing it all over. A second chance at a mask of normalcy. He wasn't rethinking or going backward. He was giving me a gift.

"I love you," I whispered through my tears. "I want you. Everything."

He slipped the ring on my finger. The diamond was huge and the color of sunshine.

"A canary diamond," he said. "For my songbird."

"Gross, Uncle Jon!"

Jonathan turned around to David, who had a face like kneaded dough at the thought.

"Yeah, gross," A laughing, grown-up voice called out. Jonathan glanced up at me for half a second, and I saw mischief in those eyes. I didn't have a moment tell him not to do whatever it was he was about to do, before he scooped up a swipe of white frosting from his cake and flung it at his tormentor.

"Quiet, Patrick!"

An impulse moved my arm, and I scooped up another bunch of frosting and flung it at my husband and fiancé, coating the bottom half of his face in a buttercream goatee.

"Be nice to the guests!"

He blew, spraying me in vanilla, and everyone laughed and clapped.

David, seeing the world as only a ten year-old could, recognized an opportunity when he saw one, and mashed his hand in the cake, then flung it at the both of us. Jonathan, not to be out-immatured, even by a ten year-old, whipped around and threw a mess of it at his nephew, missing by half, with the residual getting on Eddie.

"Hey, asshole!" Eddie shouted.

"Language!" Sheila called, too late, because her son threw another handful of cake at her. The young pitcher had great aim, getting his mother in the face with white confection.

"You!" Sheila said with a pointed finger.

I shut the cover over the piano keys just in time, because all hell broke loose. Cake flew everywhere. Laughter. Squeals. My god, the cake must have been huge. I was covered. Jonathan was covered. Everyone in my line of sight I could hit with a lump of cake was covered, laughing in the chaos through beards of white frosting and fruit filling. The kids were licking the floor. Eileen slipped on a wad of cake and laughed and her granddaughter put a handful down her shirt. Leanne fell when she tried to help her up, and Jonathan, my beautiful king, put his arms around me and kissed it off my lips.

"Goddess," he whispered, even though in the chaos of the room, he didn't have to. No one was paying attention to us.

"Yes, Jonathan. Yes. I'll marry you."

"Let's take our time." He kissed my cheek, sucking frosting off.

Our time.

He was giving me permission to stop counting the months and years. Permission to let it happen as it would, to stop using worry as a paper thin bulwark against the tides of fate. This was our time. However long it was, it belonged to us.

***

The staff had made short work of the mess. Clothing had been stripped off, some laundered, some left in bags, some rinsed and worn wet. It was probably the best party I'd been to in my life.

Sheila had loaned me a pair of pale blue velour sweatpants and a white shirt with a neck so wide it fell off my shoulder.

"I love this on you," Jonathan said, pressing his lips to my bare shoulder. We sat at the piano in the empty parlor as I played a soft jazzy thing.

"It doesn't go with the ring."

"I can't wait to see how it looks on you naked."

"It's beautiful. I love it." I did. I had a hard time keeping my eyes off it.

"I'm not trying to take away our marriage, goddess. You need to know that."

"I know."

"But it was hasty."

I sighed. Yes, it was hasty, and for all the wrong reasons, but I hadn't thought about it that deeply. I hadn't thought about anything deeply in the past six months, because it hurt, and I had the feeling that I wasn't going to be able to avoid it any more.

"I got you a birthday present," I said.

"What do you get the guy who has everything?" He brushed his lips on my shoulder and drew his fingertips along the back of my neck.

I smiled, and a ball of hitched breaths gathered in my throat. He thought he had everything. I had no idea I'd married such an optimist.

"I was supposed to play this for you in front of everyone," I said. "But you stole my limelight with this big stinking rock."

"They had a bigger one, but it was imperfect."

"It's not the size of the boat."

"Yes, it is. It's a buoyancy thing, see." He motioned with the flat of his hand in front of me, swaying it. "Too small and it sinks."

I laughed, and he laughed with me.

"Do you want to hear your song or not?"

"More than anything."

I took a deep breath. "I want you to know, I wrote one before, and it was all about what we've been through in the past six months. And I hate it. It was, I don't know. It was ugly, and it dwelled on things that weren't important."

"Can I hear it?"

"No."

I hit the first notes definitively, and found my opening tempo.

"It's short."

"Sing it twice."

"You ready, Drazen?"

"I'm ready, Drazen."

I sang it quietly, for an audience of one. I wasn't confident enough that it would survive me belting it out. Not until I did a few hundred rewrites.

How fragile it is
And how real it all feels
I can touch it, taste it
Hold it like a baby forever
But that's not the deal

I am your ever
You are my after
I am your altar
You are my prayer

Where do I end
And you begin
Because I'm untied sometimes
And we're a dandelion seed in the wind
I'm a seed or a flower.
Or I'm a breath or a wish

I am your heart
You are my beat
And I am your voice
And you are my song

"Happy birthday," I said, letting my hands slip off the keys. "Many more. Many, many more."

He kissed me, and then I kissed him. His skin smelled like cake, and his tongue tasted of salt water. We wrapped our arms around each other, connected at the mouth, as if we were passing a common soul between us.

CHAPTER 15.

JONATHAN

She was most perfect in nudity. I left her standing there, hands at her side, in front of my chair so I could watch her change without moving. I put my elbows on my knees and folded my hands together, leaning forward. She was an arm's length away, but I didn't reach for her.

"Look straight ahead, Monica."

I knew what it did to her when I kept her in stasis. I'd known the first night when I'd sent her upstairs naked, and I knew here after my birthday party, with the canary diamond heavy on her finger, that her body was changing before my eyes. In trying to stand still, she was becoming acutely aware of my gaze on her. If she stood still and I kept my concentration, she'd be soaking wet and very close before I even touched her.

Her nipples hardened in the cool night air. The triangle between her legs was a promise of compliance and unyielding pleasure. And the ocean outside the open balcony door, background noise to the melody of her cries.

Slowly, I put my hand forward and touched her belly. It quivered like the undulating ocean behind me. I drew the finger down between her legs and stroked inside her thigh. Her body reacted involuntarily, and I took my hand back.

"I'm not going to fuck you," I said. "You're already bruised everywhere I want to put my dick." I kissed her navel, then pulled away.

"My mouth is in great shape," she said.

"So is mine." I stroked her gently, awakening her nipples. "What if I laid you on that bed and pulled your legs apart. Just the tip of my tongue on

99

your cunt. If I was gentle, would you come, do you think?"

"Yes. I would."

"Do you like your ring?"

"I love it."

I stood up and wedged my foot between hers, pushing the legs apart. She was used to it, and spread them without a stumble. I went behind her. She was framed in the ocean, the curves of her ass blue and black in the evening light. I got on my knees, close to her so she could feel my breath on her. I waited until the tension was so taut it felt as if it would break like rock candy.

I brushed my finger inside her thigh. She was painted in angry bruises there. I'd stopped feeling guilty about inflicting damage, I knew the difference between hurt and harm.

"I'm sorry about the party. About worrying you. I was joking, not thinking."

"I'll die if you do that again."

I brushed my fingers over her soft, wet, lips, slightly touching the dampness there.

"I just..." she trailed off.

"Go ahead."

"That hospital. The smells. The colors. You. It claws at me. In my sleep, I hear the doctors whispering. I dream you're dying in a room I can't find. When I think of it I just think of you in pain. It hurt me. And I'm sorry I'm being self involved."

"You're not being self involved." I kissed the small of her back.

"I dread it. I know I'm going to have to go back there with you and the dread hangs on me."

I rested my cheek against the curve of her spine and put my arms around her waist. She didn't move her hands, ever obedient when in scene. I could hear her lungs through her rib cage as they let out short, sharp breaths.

"I didn't give you permission to cry," I said gently.

"I'm sorry."

I pulled away from her and stood. "On the bed, goddess. Face down. Hands under your thighs. And face the window."

She did it, and when she automatically put her ass up in ready position, my dick went completely rigid. I pressed her ass down until she was totally flat against the bed.

She watched me as I peeled my clothes off. I put pajama bottoms on so I wouldn't distract her.

"Wait here."

I went into the bathroom for lotion. The last time I'd done that I saw her negative pregnancy test. I thought about that thing every time I went in there. The burden of it was so heavy that I often went down the hall to piss.

"Are we still in scene?" she asked when I sat at the edge of the bed.

"No." I put a blob of lotion in my hand and closed it into a fist to warm it.

"I want you to fuck me."

"Nope."

"Why not?"

"Because it's my birthday, and I can do whatever I want." I put the lotion on her back and slowly dragged my hands down from her shoulder blades to her waist. He eyes fluttered closed. I put move weight on the heels of my hands and moved them back up to her shoulders.

She groaned.

"What were you and Eddie talking about?" I asked. She stiffened. "Relax. It's a rhetorical question." I worked my hands over her shoulders and down her biceps.

"There's a thing in New York. I don't think I can make it."

"No?"

She made a voice in her throat that was a cross between "no" and "that feels nice."

"The last two weeks have been good, Goddess. Really good." I focused on her shoulders for a second, then moved back down her body. I stopped at her ass, which, in all its beauty, was welted and tender. I pressed my thumbs to the sides of her spine and moved back up.

"Mmm."

"You are everything. My everything. There's nothing I'd change about you. And that includes your talent and ambition."

"I don't want to be away from you," she grumbled.

"I'm bound to you wherever you are. You know that right?"

She opened her eyes and looked at me through the web of hair. "Come with me."

"No. I have things to do here."

"Like what?"

"Hush." I moved the hair away and kissed her cheek, then grabbed the lotion and moved to the end of the bed. "You need to make your life happen. If I hadn't been sick, you'd come and go as you pleased. As *we* pleased. That's what I want for you."

The insides and backs of her thighs couldn't be touched. Her ass either. What a gorgeous mess. I'd planted that bamboo thinking I might use it, but I had no idea how effective it was. I gave her feet and calves attention, rubbing her worry and stress away.

"We need to live fully, Goddess. We both need to live as if we could die tomorrow, and we have to plan for a future where you're a hundred and ten."

She moaned. I'd promised her my mouth, and my dick wanted hers, but when I finished rubbing her feet, she was fast asleep.

CHAPTER 16.

MONICA

I called Eddie from the back deck while Jonathan had his run, and told him I was going to New York. Laurelin dropped into the lounge chair next to me in her sensible little sneakers and zip up purple fleece.

"You're going again?" she asked.

"Yeah. New York. It's a big deal, kind of. Why?"

"I have a week away coming. Jerry is taking me to—"

"You can't!" I sat up straight in my chair, tingling with adrenaline. "No, I mean. You can but not now. Please!"

"Don't worry." She put her hand on my shoulder. "I'll set him up. He'll be fine."

I wanted to support her, and I wanted her to have a nice time. I wanted Jonathan to be fine. But the reality of it wasn't making it from my brain to my mouth. No. It was taking a detour through my heart instead.

"You know what," I said, leaning back in my chair. "I'll just stay home. It's not that big a deal."

Laurelin leaned back and put her foot on the little glass and metal table. She must have thought I was schizophrenic. "You know, if this was my house, I'd never want to leave either. I'd just sit here and gestate all day."

I laughed, and she smiled at me.

"I think you can go," she said after a minute.

"Nah."

"I think you *should* go."

I didn't answer, just tilted my head a little, and she continued.

"I'm not going to be here forever, and you all need to learn how to function. I mean, these issues? The pills and the way he has to log everything? They aren't going anywhere. It's always going to be this way. And you hovering over him because you're scared, I get it. But at some point you have to let go."

I set my jaw. "I'm not letting him go."

"You know what I mean."

I did. I knew she meant I had to stop mothering him, but I'd taken it the exact wrong way because it served my immediate purpose. If I acknowledged that I knew what she meant, and that I heard it, I'd have to admit she was right.

CHAPTER 17.

JONATHAN

I ran far away. Far enough to be out of earshot and then some. I made it to the crowded part of the beach and trotted to the street, trying to shake a feeling that if Monica went to New York, things were going to get disorganized and neglected.

I'd had a mitt when I was about eleven. It was a Rawlings Gold. The best. And I wore it in just the way I liked it. One spring afternoon, I was dicking around with my cousins in the yard, tossing the ball around and trying out new curse words. We went inside to play video games, and I left my glove in the grass for a few hours like I'd done dozens of times before.

It never rains in Los Angeles, unless you leave your glove out one too many times. Then it pours, and the glove is never the same again. Just stupid negligence can turn into disaster. I got another glove, but it was never the same. My hand grew before I could wear it in right, and I always felt an acute loss I couldn't explain.

I didn't want to treat Monica like a baseball glove. I didn't want it to rain on her while my back was turned.

"Quentin?" I said when I got through to my friend. A dozen seagulls screamed at me when I interrupted them on a bench.

Quentin Marshall answered in his Aussie clip. He was a rock star specializing in charity work, and I'd written his foundation a few checks over the years. "Drazen! How are you doing? I heard about the heart, mate. That's tough stuff."

"It keeps life interesting."

"Bet it does." He paused, and I heard a siren in the distance and the belch of a city bus. Typical New York ambient. "So, what can I do for you?"

"You invited my wife to sing with you for something?"

"Yeah, I hope that's all right? She's got a great set of pipes. And the cause, could use your help as well, there. There are kids dying of dehydration every day."

"You can always count on my help. But if Monica decides to go, I want you to do something for me."

"Just say it and you got it."

How was I supposed to phrase this without sounding like a sicko stalker? I meant no harm by it, of course, and it wasn't like she hadn't travelled before, but I felt differently than I did months ago, even weeks ago.

"If there's anything she needs, or if there's something special you think she might need, even if she doesn't know what it is—can you make sure she gets it? I want her taken care of."

"That's it?"

"That's it."

"Mate, I will treat her like a precious flower. On my honor."

"Thank you."

"My pleasure."

We hung up. I watched the ocean pound the edges of the rocks into smooth stones, millennias-long process I witnessed for a few minutes before I got up and continued my run.

CHAPTER 18.

MONICA

I'd been away from post-surgery Jonathan before.
I'd flown to places I'd never been and experienced
them through hollow eyes and a worn-down heart. I
can't say my trip to New York was any different. I
was still worn out, I was still dragged home by tight-
twisted strands. I was still worried. But something
had changed. The worry wasn't colored a dark grey,
and my thoughts of Jonathan weren't painful. I
didn't feel guilty. I felt alive, vibrating, humming
with potential, and I missed him. I missed him
company, his laugh, his touch. I missed his
enfolding presence beside me. The guilt left a
vacuum in its absence, and nature, in its abhorrence,
filled it with hope.

I flew commercial. I wanted to be surrounded
by people. I wanted to feel the hum of life in the
comings and going of people, the babies crying the
pilots and stewardesses in their neat little packs,
rolling suitcases whirring behind, the bright colors
of the snack stand in the artificial lights and a
carpets worn where people walked.

I didn't make up a story when I told Jonathan I
didn't need his plane. Instead of saying something
facile about scheduling, I tried to express my need,
as intangible as it was, and he understood, and
agreed, and asked if I was going to fly coach.

That didn't seem necessary. Marrying a Drazen
had its privileges. He'd laughed and held me,
offering his team to set up the flights. As close as
we'd been in bed, or at play, or when he was
rubbing my back and telling me how much he loved
me, when I explained why I wanted to fly
commercial and he understood, I felt truly married.

He understood me. I could tell him even the worst nonsense and he did more than agree. He became a part of me, tapped into my thoughts, a partner.

I thought I knew what that meant, but I didn't.

I was so high, I chatted incessantly with the guy next to me about music and dance. He was a French choreographer, and of course he gave me a definite "I'd be happy to fuck you" vibe even after seeing my ring. But I didn't care. I wasn't sleeping with him. I could still enjoy the conversation. I was married to a king, after all. I didn't have to concern myself with what other people wanted from me.

A bodybuilder in a suit waited for me at the gate with a handwritten sign that said "Mrs. O'Drassen."

"Hi," I said. "Are you Dean?"

"Yes, ma'am." He took my bag. "I'll drive you to the hotel to drop your things. I'm hired out for as long as you need me, so you can call any time."

"Great. There's a dinner tonight? In Hell's Kitchen? Can you take me there?"

"Absolutely."

I'd never been to New York, and I couldn't believe how crowded, tight, old, and yet, shiny, spacious, vibrant it was. And this was just from out the window of a silver Rolls Royce.

Jonathan had set me up at The Stock New York, the sister hotel of the one I used to work at, citing his own hotel in the city as "too grubby." Everything was perfect. The room was huge, slick, with precisely designed proportions and windows that let onto a little patio that I wanted to sit on with my husband.

I showered and left, before I missed him more.

"Ah, I know your face!" Omar said when I showed up for the pre-studio dinner. Hartley Yallow and the Trudy Crestley were already there, and the

109

table was huge. I was wrung out from the flight, but too excited to sleep.

"I know yours, too," I said. Everyone knew it. He had classic South American good looks that came from an Argentinian mother and an Italian father. His voice, however, was something no genetic pairing could create.

I sat down and we ordered. More people came. I could hardly keep up with the names, because even though I knew them all I was overwhelmed and in love with that moment. Ivan Braf showed up with this wife and I envied her presence. I wanted Jonathan, his company next to me, even if he didn't say a word. It wasn't that I was stealing moments before his death, it was only that I wanted this moment to be complete, and without him, it wasn't.

But it was good. Very good. Quentin Marshall showed up with the guys from The Breakfront.

"Monica Faulkner," Quentin said in his thick Aussie accent. "So happy you could come. Now we all have to take our game up a notch."

He wagged his finger around the table.

"Oh, I don't think—"

"We need her on the chorus," Omar said, pointing his fork. "Flat out."

"*You* were on the chorus," Quentin replied.

"I—" I couldn't finish a denial.

"There's no point having her here unless you showcase her voice," Omar argued.

"That's true," Quentin replied.

"Hang on!" I said, putting my fist down. I didn't watch for their reaction, because I knew I didn't have a second before they'd interrupt. "Even if all this is true, it's irrelevant. My name isn't going to sell the record, and the point is to *sell the record.*

Nobody knows me, so showcasing me gets you nowhere."

"She has a point," Trudy said. I nodded to her and she nodded back.

"Fine!" Quentin proclaimed. "We rehearse tomorrow and try it out. Once Victory Spontaine gets in, whenever that is, we decide once and for all." He clacked the ice at the bottom of his glass. "My drink is empty." He twisted in his seat to look for a waiter.

I hadn't realized until that moment that the rest of the restaurant found the gathering at our table very interesting. Black rectangles hovered over heads, and little phone flashes went off. The dinner was publicity. I hadn't thought of that. I wished I'd worn lipstick or done something with my hair.

Omar, who was next to me, leaned close. "I'm fighting for you to get the chorus."

"Why?"

"Because you have the most unique voice I've ever heard."

I swallowed. "Well, my point stands."

"If we want to sell the record, it has to be a *great record.* That's the number one priority."

I couldn't believe he was saying this to me. Omar D'Alessio. Holy shit. I couldn't believe he was even talking to me.

"You're pretty great, Omar."

"I never said I wasn't." He put his arm around me. "But there's room for another." He kissed me on the cheek, and I felt accepted as a musician and artist. Jonathan was the only thing missing from that moment. I wished he could have seen it.

CHAPTER 19.

JONATHAN

Laurelin puttered around the kitchen putting
ingredients into two blender jars that were meant to
hold me for two days. She put measured portions of
vitamins, greens, milk, powdered puke, and dried
shit into a healthful grotesquerie of layers that
would be in the fridge for my reluctant
consumption.

I didn't have to think about it. I just had to
blend it and choke on it. She'd already taken my
blood pressure (one ten over seventy), drawn blood
(a monthly task), and hooked me up to an EKG
(looked good). The meds for the week were set out
so I didn't have to count. The privilege of money. I
could pay someone to keep me from the
mundanities of my illness.

"Where's he taking you?" I asked.

"We're driving up to Monterey," she replied in a
singsong. "Donny is staying with grandma, so it's
kind of a last hurrah before I get huge."

"Good for him."

"I have everything you need here until
Wednesday. Then you follow this list on the fridge
to make new. I'd make them for you for the whole
ten days but the ingredients are perishable."

"I wish they'd perish." I said it in passing just to
make the joke. I was looking at the news on a tablet
and was on humor autopilot.

"Oh stop. Be cheerful." I looked up at her to
see her holding up her finger. "Twenty years ago,
you'd be the one who perished. And when you
complain, people think you won't do with you're
supposed to when they're gone."

She winked and went back to arranging my fridge.

"Are you trying to tell me something?"

"Attitude is everything." More lilting vowels to express something serious. "You missed a few days in your log," she flicked her wrist at my little blue leather book. "You need to take it with you everywhere. Even if you're going to a restaurant." I rolled my eyes and immediately felt like an adolescent or worse. I ran through the international news as if the tablet was on fire, trying to not feel over mothered. I hired her to do this. I couldn't get mad about it.

"Okay," was all I could get out.

"What is this?" She took a plastic container out of the crisper and held it at my eye level.

I looked at it, then back to the tablet. "Monica's Brazilian chimichuri. Her mother was over the other night. The two of them ate it like...I don't know." I waved my hand. "They slather it on everything like they're trying to scald their faces. It's blowtorch hot."

"Oh, that sounds good."

"Does spicy food bother you? With the pregnancy?"

"Nope."

"Take it, then." I scrolled through the financials. "We have two."

"Really?" She peeled the top off and took a whiff. "Oh my God this smells so good."

She put it under my nose and I pushed her away. "Oh," she said. "I forgot. Well, I understand. Donny doesn't like spicy food either." She put the container in her bag of medicinal crap.

"Donny's three," I said.

Laurelin shrugged. "He's a good boy." She patted my shoulder. "Like you."

I didn't want to fuck my nurse at all. Not even a little. But I wanted to spank her. Hard.

I turned back to my tablet, and tapped the local news, missed and hit entertainment, which I couldn't care less about. But I let it load, and probably because Monica's name was associated with my account, or the wifi, or because it was the top entertainment story of the minute to people who weren't married to her, her picture was front and center.

Her and some swarthy guy. His arm was around her. He was kissing her cheek at a restaurant, and she was smiling, looking at the ceiling. She looked happy and carefree. In her element. And on his face? This was a simple prelude to fucking her. I couldn't take my eyes off the picture, that look in his eye. His fingertip on her shoulder as if testing his right to touch her.

I knew my wife didn't have cheating in her heart. But I also knew men, and this asshole had her body on his mind. He wanted to fuck her. My wife. Mine. I wanted to take his skin and peel it off him. Rip him apart.

"Mister Drazen?"

Laurelin's voice sounded a million miles away. "What?"

"Are you all right?"

I tore my face from the screen and looked at her. Her brow was knit, and she was packed to go.

"I'm fine."

"I think I should take your BP again."

"No, no. I'm fine. Let me walk you out."

I smiled, but I knew no joy reached my eyes. I hustled her to the front door.

"Mister Drazen," she said when we got there. "Really, you need to avoid stress."

"Stress is part of life. Don't worry. I'm good."

She left. I went upstairs and paced. Looked at my watch. Did some math. I couldn't keep Monica enclosed. I couldn't keep men from wanting her. She only got more beautiful every day, and men were disgusting creatures who cared for nothing but the daily mounting pressure in their ball sacks.

I trusted her. With every cell in my body I trusted her. But when I thought about how I'd almost lost her, how she hadn't been happy and I just kept letting shit slide, I wondered what would have happened if I hadn't gone to the studio that day and reasserted myself.

She could be away. She could travel. Her career was necessary to her happiness, and more than anything, I wanted her to be happy.

So why did that picture bother me? We'd reestablished ourselves. I trusted her. She needed to do her job and make her art. What was the problem?

The problem was that there was a disconnect, and that disconnect was me. She'd come back to me fully, but I hadn't broached my side of the distance. I hadn't gone to her with an open heart the way she'd come to me.

That was going to change.

CHAPTER 20.

MONICA

The balcony had room for two, maybe three if everyone liked each other. It overlooked a tiny street in Chinatown, down a cobblestone street and onto the tops of the beat down signs in Cantonese. Manhattan had many of the same structures as Los Angeles. They were straight up from the ground at ninety degrees, had corners, straight walls, windows and roofs. Some buildings were made well and some were sad. But the whole proportion of the place was different. It wasn't absorbed by car, it could only be experienced on foot or bike, and then the flower boxes, cornerstones and cobbled streets took on their natural life.

I had no business being out there, since Omar and Trudy were smoking and I wasn't about to even try it.

"It gives me my edge," Omar said. "Biggest secret in music, how many of us smoke."

"The other type of smoke, not such a secret," Trudy said. She was a guitarist, and could smoke her brains out for all I cared. From Omar, well, I admitted to being a little disappointed. I took so much care with my vocal chords. I could tell when there was a forest fire in Flintridge based on how my throat felt.

"Does he do this all the time?" I jerked my head toward the inside, where Hartley had abandoned his drums to throw up last night's party.

Trudy smashed her cigarette underfoot and blew a cloud carelessly. It landed in my face, and I resisted the urge to wave my hand in front of me.

"Constantly," she said. "But he never pukes. I think it's a flu or something."

"Oh." I tried to not look more worried than any normal person would. Normal people got the flu and just suffered through it. I had a husband on immunosuppressants, and a flu could kill him.

"Quentin's looking for another one." Omar shrugged. "Or Franco can do it."

"Nope," Trudy said. "He's down with it."

"What is it? A percussionist's strain?" I joked.

"All those guys hang out together. It's like incest without the sex."

I don't know what came over me, but my words shot out of my mouth before I even thought about the logistics of it.

"I know one," I said. "He can be here tomorrow. He has something today. He's really good."

"Do I know him?"

"He's from LA originally. So, probably not. He's super hot in indie circles."

"Not that husband of yours is it?" Omar smiled a half moon of perfect white piano keys. It was the third time he's mentioned Jonathan that day, as if he was trying to gauge my reactions.

"The only instrument Jonathan plays is me."

"That can be good or bad."

"He's a maestro, trust me."

I went inside. I'd wanted to learn from Omar, and he'd taught me a few things. but I was starting to feel as if it all came with a price. Maybe that price was simple flirtation and attention, or maybe he expected more, but I was getting irritated with his off color comments and sultry eyeballing.

Everyone was filing back into the studio. There were fifteen actual musicians. Some kept klatches of preeners and hangers. Others traveled alone. Add to that the engineers, press, security and agents, and the room was hot as a sweatbox and smelled only ten percent better.

I couldn't believe there wouldn't be a drummer among us, but it was worth a try. I found Quentin in the middle of eating a slab of crunchy fried fish, surrounded by people I didn't know.

"Hey," I said, trying to slink into the tiny room unobtrusively and failing.

"Faulkner!" he said. "Everyone out!" he made shoo shoo motions with his fingers and everyone shooed. He closed the door behind them. I hoped I wasn't stepping out of the frying pan with Omar and into the fire with Quentin.

"Sorry," he said, rooting around his leather messenger bag. "Not a big deal I just didn't know what this was so I didn't want to give it to you in front of everyone." He handed me a long, blue velvet box. "This was at reception with your name on it."

"Thank you," I said, taking it.

He slung the bag over his shoulder. "We're done today. I have to find a drummer."

"No one in this building can do percussion? It's a house full of musicians."

"You have no idea how hard it is to find a good one."

"I kind of do.."

"Evan Arden's in the bathroom puking his guts out, and he's on bass. I think we're finished for the day." He made motions to leave, but was so slow about it. He glanced at the velvet box, then back at me. "Sorry, not trying to be nosy."

"Not trying?"

"Even straight guys like a little sparkle. Come on. Don't hold out."

I smiled. What could it be? Jonathan never disappointed me, but I was afraid it was a diamond-studded leather collar or a bracelet with the word SLAVE in emeralds. That might require a little more explaining than I was willing to do.

I held the box open to eye level and cracked it open so only I could see. Whatever it was, it didn't sparkle. I didn't know if that excited me or scared me. But it looked harmless enough. I opened it all the way.

"What is it?" he said, hand on the doorknob.

"It's a Sharpie."

I turned it to him. Indeed, right inside the bracelet box, lay a black Sharpie. I could see from his expression that it was a disappointment, as if he expected an actual bracelet in the bracelet box.

"What's it for?"

"I have no idea."

I opened the little card that had been folded inside the lid. It was typed.

Keep this with you, Goddess.

I closed it slowly.

"That's not just a Sharpie," Quentin said. "Probably the first step to some game. He's more of a romantic than I thought."

"You know him?"

"We have a long history of feeding children together."

"Is that why you hired me?" I said it before I could catch it. It was completely unprofessional to ask such a thing. It made me look like an insecure ingrate.

"I hired you because Dionne Harber couldn't make it." He winked. "I don't regret it." He winked at me and got away with it. "If tomorrow is cancelled I'll send a group text."

"Thanks."

He left with a smile. I opened the velvet box again. Shook it. Looked under it. Turned the card over. Nothing special. I got my stuff to go.

Typically, when I travelled, Jonathan and I spoke once a day and the conversations were short and mostly about his medicines and appointments. But that was the old us. The miserable us. The couple treading water in a sea of doubt and unsaid truths. I didn't know or understand the couple we'd become, and I didn't think there was much precedent for it.

So, I didn't know what he intended with the permanent marker, and I didn't know enough to be excited, or anxious. I was only curious as we laid down some tracks, and I played my theramin for everyone in the studio while we waited for two other people to decide if they were too sick to continue.

"We're doing a small thing at a club after," Omar whispered in the hall outside the bathrooms. "You're invited."

"Thank you. I think I'm just going to bed."

"Alone? We have the day off tomorrow, you know." He put his hand on my wrist.

"You know I'm married, right Omar?"

"Where is he?" He spread his arms, indicating the whole of the studio, New York, the world about us, where Jonathan wasn't. Was he drunk? Who would make such an implication? What person in their right mind would assume my husband's presence was required for my fidelity?

And it came to me in the tightness of Omar's jaw and the tension in his fingers. He was on something. Some white substance that whispered in his ear that he was a god and entitled to whatever he felt like having today. I sighed. I'd really admired him. He sang like an angel, but he'd just been in the studio thirty minutes ago, and if I recalled the moments of inappropriate laughter and long space-outs where I thought he was preparing, he'd been stoned the whole time. I knew how many artists worked stoned and I'd always told myself it was their thing, and not my business, but suddenly I felt as if it was most certainly my business.

"My husband's home," I said, "waiting for me to call."

He looked at me like he didn't believe me.

"Look," I continued, "I know what you've probably heard about me, and it may be all true. But this scene, the drugs and the other shit? The partying until all hours? The fucking around? It's not my thing. And if that means I'll always be small time, well, it's okay."

He didn't move, as if stuck in that moment.

"You think I got where I am because I party?"

"No, I—"

"No?" he interrupted.

I didn't think he'd coasted. Not at all. But he wasn't interested in hearing it. I'd insulted his talent and his manhood, and he was walking away with at least one intact.

"Break it down," he said firmly, his jaw still grinding. "You just said you'd be small time if you didn't party. You know what, girl, I've done everything I could to support you. I lifted you up the minute you got here. And this is the attitude you throw me? You think your pussy is dipped in gold? Well, fuck you."

121

He turned on his heel and went down the hall just as Rob Devon cut the turn and ran into the men's room as if his belly was on fire. In seconds, the hallway was silent again.

I dragged myself out the door, and Dean waited for me in the Rolls. I'd walked into the studio wrapped in confidence and love and I was walking out feeling as if my expensive ride was an ugly appendage. A street sign pointing to my gold-plated cunt. God, I must make such a scene with this stupid car.

"Mrs. Drazen," Dean said by way of greeting.

"Hi, Dean."

"Back to the hotel?" He opened the back door.

"Yes, thanks."

I slid in to the pristine comfort of the Rolls. It envelops you, this luxury. The money. The sense of well-being. That was the point, wasn't it? When the car started there was no jolt, no rumble, just movement.

I called Jonathan as the streetlights streaked across the night sky, then stopped seamlessly at a stop sign, then started again.

"Hello, Monica," he said, and I wanted to cry.

"Hi."

"I see you're on your way back to the hotel?"

"Is this Dean telling your everything or do you have a tracking device on me?"

"Yes to both. How are you?"

"Do you know, the Rolls doesn't even obey the law of inertia? Like when Dean stops at the light, my body doesn't go forward a little and when he starts again, I can feel it going, but it's not like I feel my back against the seat, even? Did you know that?"

"I never noticed."

We went through a busy part of town and I curled into the seat, watching the Saturday night crowds walk the streets. People crossing stared at the car, big packs and smaller groups, dressed for big things, made up for the lights and sounds, a single wave in an ocean of revelry.

"Did you get my present?" he said.

"Yes. I love it. How did you know I needed to write my name on all my tags?"

"Are you all right?"

"What time is it there?"

"Sun's just thinking about setting."

"Is it hot? Is it gloomy? Tell me things."

"It's nice. It's mid June. Same as always. The marine layer burned off and I can see....let me look...one two three four five clouds out the kitchen window. One is shaped like a rabbit. One is shaped like a guitar. It makes me think of you."

"What about the other three? What are they shaped like?"

"Big white turds."

I laughed.

"Did you take your medicine?"

"Yes, mom."

"And drink your shit shake?"

"Yes."

"And did you go for a run?"

"Yes. You never answered my question. Are you all right?"

I sighed. I knew he could hear it. I wanted him to.

"I feel, I guess, not lonely. Not alone. Just, separate. Separate from you and separate from everyone here. It's...I can't pin it down. I guess it's not a bad feeling as much as it's a weird,

123

disconnected feeling. Uncomfortable. I don't know."

I could hear him breathing, and the lawn mower outside our house, and the birds in Los Angeles.

"Would you believe me if I said I know how you feel?"

"Yeah."

Dean pulled up to the hotel. A doorman in a snazzy uniform was ready to open the door before the car stopped without a jolt. The inside of the hotel through the glass windows looked gilded and soft, as if the lights were colored gold.

"Do you have your marker?" Jonathan asked.

"Of course. I'll treasure it always."

"Hang up with me then, and call back on the tablet. I want to see you."

Dean opened the door for me, and I hung up.

CHAPTER 21.

MONICA

Jonathan was in the process of transferring his hotel on the Lower East Side. Hotel D, on Avenue D. His fourth and a huge risk. He shook his head whenever he talked about it. He said it was too small for me. Too old, too trendy, too loud; he had a million reasons why I should stay at The Stock. A few minutes though, and I knew why he'd kept me away from D. He didn't think it was safe. Who even knew why. He'd been known for putting beautiful hotels in up and coming neighborhoods like canaries in a coal mine. Maybe this little bird hadn't gotten out.

The Stock had every imaginable trend-forward trapping. Wool rugs with barely discernible patterns that looked like they'd been through a war zone in exactly the right places. Maple and mahogany paneling. Blackened brass chandeliers with frosted glass shades that curved in ways that were surprising and yet, inevitable. Good-looking staff in sharp uniforms.

"It's a parody of itself," I said when I called him from my suite. In the screen of the tablet, I could see he'd moved out to the side patio overlooking the twinkling grid of the city. "Or a farce. I can't decide which." I pouted at him from the edge of the bed.

"I'll tell Sam you said so."

"I wanted to stay in D." I snapped the drapes open. Manhattan was dark, and vibrant and closed tight in a granite and clay brick embrace.

"It's in Alphabet City. There's piss in the doorways from the seventies. I already don't like you spending days in a studio in Chinatown."

"A little grit's kind of nice."

"Nice?" He leaned forward in his seat.

"Yeah, nice." I opened the patio door, holding my tablet out so he could see me.

"Turn the camera around," he said. "Show me the view."

I did, then showed him the street below and the building across Lexington. "Not much to speak of," I said. "Except, yeah. New York's kind of fabulous."

"Go back inside."

I turned the tablet and looked back at him in his dying-daylight rectangle. I knew where I was in relation to his eyes, and if he was looking at me, he'd be looking slightly off camera. He was looking directly into the lens, which was right above the screen, and though the mic was tiny and tinny, I knew I was hearing his dominant voice.

"Put the tablet on the desk so I can see you."

I leaned it against the lamp. There was something ridiculous about seeing him inside that rectangle with our backyard behind him. In the top right corner of the screen a small box showed what he saw as I stood there. My face was off screen. I was only visible from neck to knees.

"Take your clothes off," he said, casually yet firmly, as if asking me to pass the salt. As if it was no more than a courtesy to ask for what should be available to him without question.

I pulled my t-shirt over my head, and watched myself take off my bra. My breasts bounced out, and I could see my hard nipples in the screen. Jonathan was impassive, tapping his thumbs together as if keeping a rhythm.

I peeled my pants off, down to the lace thong I wore for him in his absence. I let him see it for a second, but he twisted his hand at the wrist in a "get on with it" motion. I got them off and stood before the tablet, naked neck to knees.

"Are you wet?" he asked.

"Yes."

"Check for me."

I put my hand between my legs. I saw it slipping down my belly in the screen. Saw the way my knees bent a little when I spread my legs to accept my fingers.

"I'm wet," I said.

"Put your fingers in your mouth. And let me see."

I bent to look at him, lips puckered around my fingers, tongue curled around them, the pungent, sordid, sexy taste of my cunt filling my mouth. His eyes warmed with arousal.

"Go get the pen," he said.

I plucked it off the desk and showed him.

"Put the pen in your mouth. Get the desk chair. Sit in it and put your feet on the desk. I want to see your beautiful cunt."

I wheeled the chair over, placing it in front of the desk. He waited, fingers laced together on the ipad screen. He was casual and intense at the same time, as if he didn't have to worry about me doing what he asked. He was just going to wait.

I put my feet up on the desk, exposing myself to him. I could see myself on the little corner of the screen, the soft part of me, the place where I was split in two, the fold of sensation in between the smooth mass of skin, and I was shocked by the sight of it.

"That's mine," he said. "You understand, my wife, that everything I see there is mine?"

"Yes."

"You're wet, and that's mine, too. No matter where you are, I own your cunt."

"It's yours. It's only for you. It's so wet for you."

"Mark it," he said.

It took me a second to understand. Even with the sharpie in my teeth, then, seeing my thighs against the wet flesh between them, I knew what he meant.

I popped the base free of the cap, and leaned over, drawing a big "J" on my left inner thigh. Glancing up at him, he gave a slight shake of his head.

"You start on your right, at the knee."

I switched and pulled the skin to make it taut for the marker. Like his fingers, it was firm and purposeful, like his tongue, it was damp and warm.

"Wherever you are," he said low and steady as I wrote his name, knee to crotch. "I own you. I own your filthy mouth. I own your dirty mind. When you get wet thinking about fucking, it's mine. Every drop from you. I own your every thought. You are my property."

I looked back at him. My breath was short. And when I saw myself, the flesh between my legs now exposed, wet, swollen and "Jonathan's" marked on my inner thigh, a bolt of pleasure ran through me.

"This is crazy," I gasped. "I'm going to come."

"Not until you finish the other side."

"Okay." I didn't know if I was going to make it.

"No touching."

What was I supposed to put on the other side? I couldn't think. I glanced up at him. A shadow of a smirk crossed his lips.

I started with the letter "P" a few inches from my center, the pen tip becoming him, his body, his intention, his attention, the tingling a wall of sensation as I spelled "Property" down my leg. As I put the leg on the Y, the pressure had build up so much I knew I didn't have long.

"Look at yourself," he said.

"I'll come if I do."

"No, you won't. Not until I say."

But I didn't. I just looked at the marks between my legs. I was owned. Property. Without desire or ambition, a slave without responsibility or longing. Free.

"Look, Monica," he said sternly, and I looked. Jonathan's Property.

"Yes," I said, flooded now with a tsunami of an orgasm, pushing at the walls of my control. "You own me. I am your subject." I could barely speak through the throb. "You are my master."

"I'm going to put my cock inside you, everywhere, and I'm not going to ask first. You're going to spread your legs and submit yourself. Your mouth. Your cunt. Your tight little ass. I'm going to hurt you. I'm going to crack you open and suck you dry."

"Oh, god when you talk like that." Every word rushed me to orgasm, but like the door at the end of the hall in a movie, it got closer and further at the same time. Juice dripped over my ass. How long would he do this?

"I am yours," I said, because I wanted to say "let me come,"

"Put your fingers inside yourself."

I slid two fingers in me and groaned.

"Shh. Over your clit. But don't come yet."

I didn't know how it would be possible. My clit was swollen and soaked. I touched it gently.

"Would you like to come?" he asked.

"Yes, please."

"Move your fingers very slowly, and don't make a sound. I want to see how your body moves."

I moved my finger in circles.

"Slower, not enough to come. Not yet."

But it didn't matter. I was on the edge. The dam burst and I came, first bending over, moth open, face rigid, then arching my back until I was leveraged on the edge of the desk and thrusting my pussy at the camera.

When I came down, looking at him with my hair disheveled and my hand cupping the throbbing mass between my legs, I smiled, and he shook his head.

"You are in so much trouble," he said.

"I'm sorry, I couldn't—"

"No talking. Just, when I see you, be ready for the spanking of your young life."

He winked and cut the call. I was left staring at a dead iPad.

I wanted to go home. I wanted his arms around me, his sharp scent, his cruel hands and unforgiving mouth. I held my phone as if I was testing its weight. I could book a flight right now and show up naked on the doorstep.

But what if the tightness in my stomach was the flu? Everyone was getting it. The feeling in my stomach didn't feel like any flu I'd ever had, because it was just tight. No more, no less. Like a butterfly's torn ligament. But if I had it, I couldn't go home.

Between my legs, the words *Jonathan's Property* was scrawled in Sharpie. I was his, and I wanted to go home to him. Could I go home day after tomorrow for a weekend? And if so, should I? I could have this flu. I could be carrying. No. I couldn't go. I couldn't risk his health, because complications were a cotton candy funnel, rolling around the edge of the drum. It looks like nothing, then not too much, then an insane cloud of pink sugar before you even blink, and we were dying at Sequoia.

I couldn't go home if I was sick.

The phone buzzed right in my hand. It was Quentin.

—Omar's got it. We're off
for a week—
I could go now. Tomorrow.

—Ok got it—

I tapped the phone to my upper lip, looking out over Lexington Avenue. So many people everywhere, in a city that never sleeps.

—Do you have the number for a
doctor who keeps late hours?—

—Sure. You all right?—

How should I answer that? I didn't want to tell him I was going home. I was still too new, too replaceable to even talk about taking a risk. Besides, he knew Jonathan.

—I'm fine just want to see if I
have this flu thing. I want to go
home and can't be sick. Pls don't
tell Jonathan it's a surprise—

An address and number came through. I believed I was being diligent about my husband's health, but I knew that no matter what the doctor said, I was going home. I'd rather talk to Jonathan through a wall than a phone line.

CHAPTER 22.

JONATHAN

I cut the call because I was frustrated and I couldn't show it. That wasn't good enough. Her willful obedience drove me to distraction, and her accidental disobedience made my palms sting with the longing for the sting of her ass under them. I wanted to mark her with my own hand. Make her come with my body. Fill her with myself, and here I was in my kitchen, with a dick hard enough to crack the granite countertop.

This wasn't working. A thousand times this wasn't working.

And why? Because I didn't want to travel. Because the thought of being too far from Sequoia froze me solid. And a plane? I couldn't get the image of my heart jumping from of my chest out of my mind, and the thought of isolating myself on a plane made that image play and replay until the organ squeaked out a puddle of blood in the leather seat.

But being away from her wasn't working either. She was getting recognized for her talent, and that meant she was becoming desirable to a certain kind of asshole. She was trustworthy. I didn't have to assert myself. I didn't have to lay claim on her. I was an intelligent man with a wife who had laid down her life for him. I could reason my way into the knowledge that she'd never betray me. I could feel the fidelity in her heart.

But I did need to assert myself, and the thought of men who wanted to fuck her breathing the same air as her made me boil. I was a child. An unreasonable, hateful brat.

All true. And so what?

I was hungry, and the fridge was empty of anything I wanted. I snapped out my box of pills and the last jar of chimichuri.

If staying close to her and keeping those men off her meant I got on a plane and went where she went and did what she did, then my anxieties about traveling were going to have to just shut the fuck up. I took a handful of pills and choked it down with warm tap water. Then another, swallowing more frustration than vitamins, more anger than medicine. My body was going to reject this heart just because my mind was rejecting everything I'd held onto for months.

That picture with Omar. If I trusted her, why had it burned me? Why did it feel like a punch in the gut?

Because I'd left her alone. I'd deserted her. She didn't need a leash. She didn't need a reminder of her vows or commitments, but I'd assumed she didn't need or want my presence, and I'd accepted that because it had been convenient for me. I didn't have to go anywhere if I made it her fault I wasn't going. I'd been responsible for that picture and the state of our current discontent.

I ripped open a bag of bread and jammed it in the chimichuri. The oil and flakes of parsley dripped off it. The peppers were invisibly green in the mix, and I didn't give a fuck. I ate it. Cringed. God, that chemical burn. How could I have eaten stuff this hot and not needed a skin graft after? How could this not be damaging tissue? I smelled flesh burning and knew it was in my mind. I curled the bread on itself and scooped up more, eating it before the burn from the last bite had dissipated.

I didn't swallow. I kept it in my mouth, nurturing it, letting it hurt me, rejecting whatever weakness this new heart had brought, because they were reactions to something that happened to someone else. They weren't me. I had the opportunity and responsibility to reject the changes I didn't want, and god damnit, this was excellent chimichuri.

I ate it, leaning over the counter, until the last flake of parsley was gone and my eyes teared. And as if all the new traits I'd gained feared I'd leave, I had the desire to go for a run.

"That, I'm keeping," I said as I dropped the empty jar into the sink. "I like it."

I laced up my sneakers and took my phone, because this run was going to have a purpose. I had no more excuses.

In the middle the run, as I was whipping wet sand, I slowed to a walk and called Dr. Solis.

"He's with a patient," his assistant said. "Should he call you back?"

She'd presented me with the perfect opportunity to bail. The call might not go through, or maybe I wouldn't pick up. If he called back late enough, I wouldn't be able to get Jacques online in time for a flight plan.

"I'll wait."

"Is this an emergency, Mr. Drazen?"

"No. Yes, but no."

I faced the darkening ocean, watching the last of the sun dip into the horizon. I heard the birds overhead, and had a flash of my heart jumping out of my chest and splatting on the wet sand before a wave came in. The weight of the heart was enough to dig it into the sand, and create a wake of ripples as it fought, still beating, to stay on the beach against the pressure of the water. I stared at the spot, feeling an emptiness in my chest as two seagulls came down and plucked it up, fighting for the fresh meat.

"Fuck you," I said. "You're not real."

"Jon? What's the trouble?" Dr. Solis said, jarring me.

"I need to travel."

"So?"

"Cross country."

"Tell Patty the city. She'll notify the nearest cardiac unit and text you a number. Is that what this was about?"

I swallowed. No, that wasn't what it was about. It was about paralyzing fear that I didn't recognize because it was so foreign. It was about my wife, and how I'd abandoned her because of that fear. It was about regret, and forgiveness, and worthiness.

"Yeah," I said. "That was it."

"Good," he said and hung up without another word. Damned doctors. Hold a human heart in your hand and the everyday courtesies go out the window. I laughed to myself. I was going to New York.

CHAPTER 23.

MONICA

"Can you explain this one more time?" the old doctor asked with an accent so deeply New Yawk he sounded like an old Irish cop in a black and white movie. The office was in the eighties and Seventh Avenue, with old cabinets, ancient metal and glass syringes in frames, and photos of a family, then a family's family. The certificates and diplomas, if observed closely, were from the fifties.

I sat on the leather-surfaced examining table with my hands folded in my lap. "My husband is immunosuppressed—"

"I got that part." The doctor moved his half-moon glasses to the top of his bald head. "I'll be happy to help you, but if you're not actually sick..." He pivoted his hand at the wrist.

"I can't bring the flu home."

"Do you have any symptoms?"

"My stomach is a little ishy."

"Vomiting? Diarrhea?"

"No."

"So, go home."

I made a face and twisted my shoulders. I don't know what I was trying to express but discomfort and awkwardness.

"Do you not want to go home? Does he beat you?"

"No!" He did, of course, but that wasn't what the good doctor meant. "I'm worried. If I get him sick, it's not like a normal person getting sick. He had a heart transplant."

The doctor held his hand up. It was surprisingly big, like a wrinkled leather dinner plate.

"I tell you what. You're a nervous wreck. I can see it. And you're blood pressure's through the roof. You gave Bernice a urine sample when you came in?"

"No, I—."

"Do that, then. We'll check your sugar. Check for antibodies. If there's anything irregular, I'll let you know. You might be carrying a virus anyway, and you might not. There's not much more I can do."

"That's fine. It's great. Thank you!"

"You're very cute, young lady. If I were about sixty years younger, I'd be the older man in your life."

I laughed, and he helped me off the table with his dinner plate hands.

I gave my sample and waited.

What would I do if I came back with some sign that something was not a hundred percent? Like elevated blood sugar? Could mean my body was fighting something, and could mean I ate too much bread with lunch. Would I stay in New York to keep Jonathan safe? Or would I go home and tell him to stay away from me?

I'd been sick only once since the surgery, at the end of February. It had been a cold that kept me out of the studio, and as frustrating as that was, it also meant I was relegated to another bedroom until Laurelin cleared me to touch my husband. I cursed her. I yelled at her. I told her that I was leaving for Corfu in three days and I was entitled to see Jonathan before then.

And she reminded me that by infecting him with a cold, I'd send him right back to Sequoia Hospital faster than if I hit him over the head with a two-by-four.

That shut me up.

I was smiling about it when the good doctor appeared from behind his shellacked wood door.

"Mrs. Faulkner?"

I didn't correct him. "Yes?"

"Congratulations. We've found the source of your ishy stomach."

CHAPTER 24.

JONATHAN

The night I decided to shed the yoke of love I carried for my ex-wife, I'd felt so unburdened I laughed. When I let go of my fear of travelling, I didn't laugh quite as hard, but I walked home quickly, smiling the whole way.

"Mira!" I said when I saw her. "Pack me some things, would you?"

"Sure sure. How long for?"

"Few days." If I stayed longer I could have the hotel launder, or buy new. It didn't matter. Nothing mattered but getting out of this old skin of a house and into my wife's.

"Business or pleasure?"

"Pleasure! A little chilly. Los Angeles in November-ish."

She smiled widely. "Yes, sir. When are you leaving?"

"Immediately. Go. Jeans and shirts. Two sweaters. Go."

Aling Mira trotted upstairs when I remembered something. "Mira!"

She leaned over the banister. "Sir?"

"Two leather belts. One narrow, one wide."

"What color?"

"Doesn't matter."

She nodded and went upstairs. I got on the phone.

"Jacques?"

"Hello, Mister Drazen."

"I need to go to New York."

"When?"

"Now."

I was greeted by an unusual pause.

"What?" I said.

"I'm calculating how long it will take to get there."

"From where?"

"We just got into Chicago."

"With the plane?" I started my own calculations.

"For the Prima Culture conference, you—"

"Signed off. Shit." I stood in the middle of the living room and rubbed my eyes. When I'd stopped flying I'd freely loaned the plane to anyone on my staff who needed it for business, and months ago my executive group had requested it. So, the Gulfstream was in Chicago, which was three flying hours. An hour getting a flight plan approved, half an hour prep. Three hours in the air. Redoing it all once he hit Santa Monica and the last, most unmovable of obstacles, pilot exhaustion. If he just flew into Chicago today and came right back, he wouldn't be able to legally pilot the plane to New York.

"I can get back but then I can't take you."

When did I decide to start hiring such law-abiding staff? Was I going to have to jog to New York?

"Is Petra with you?"

"She's with the baby." I'd hit some nerve. I heard it in the edge in his voice. Petra had given birth to their little boy, Claude weeks ago. Jacques had been manning the plane on his own, which was completely legal and fine up until then. At that moment, it had become a pain in the ass.

"Do you have a nanny?" I asked, knowing the answer.

"She's breastfeeding, Mister Drazen. I'm sorry. She can't pilot to New York and back without feeding him."

141

I thought there might be answers that had to do with latex nipples and breast pumps, but I knew nothing about it, and for his part, Jacques probably would have suggested it if it had been a possibility.

And did I need to go, really? What was going to happen if I waited a day? Exactly nothing? No lives or livelihoods were at stake. But having decided I wasn't afraid, that I was ready to go anywhere with her, I couldn't wait another second.

"Listen," I said. "I am being a nightmare of a boss, and the fact that I admit it isn't going to soften this. I need you to get home and I need Petra to fly that plane. Get a freelance copilot or a nanny, on me, but I need to go."

"Mister Drazen. We won't hire a nanny. That's not how we do it."

What I enjoyed about Jacques was that he'd never asked me why I suddenly had to go anywhere. He just flew the damned plane. In return, I couldn't ask him what kind of stupid fucking rule prevented him from taking care of his son while Petra sat in the cockpit.

I plopped back on the couch, and put my feet on the coffee table, stretching my legs, tensing and releasing.

"How long in the air between here and New York? Five hours? Six?"

"Yes. But—"

"I have an idea. Just hear me out."

CHAPTER 25.

MONICA

I snapped the hotel door shut behind me and ran to the bathroom, stripping as I went. The mirror in the deluxe suite went from floor to ceiling seamlessly, and made me look sickly skinny. So when I got in front of it and turned to the side, I felt the same, or worse, because I was two months knocked up and to me, I still looked like bag of bones.

"You have to start eating," I reprimanded myself. "Someone else is counting on you."

I surprised myself. What was I doing? I didn't want a baby. I wanted to just make Jonathan as comfortable and happy as possible for however long he had. That was it. Not raise children into orphanhood.

I breathed heavily, and tilted one leg. Inside the thigh, the word *Jonathan's* became visible at the bottom. I was marked, written on, branded with his name. I closed my eyes, and wondered what I'd prayed for.

Was I relieved? Disappointed? What would change? Would I throw caution to the wind and let my sons and daughters go through puberty with a brave and dead father? What was I agreeing to?

I didn't know. But I knew things were going to change. If we were having a baby, then fuck it, I'd just deal with it.

A smile stretched across my face as if it was someone else's. I felt the muscles tense and expand, felt the swelling in my heart one felt when one smiled with joy. It was as if deciding to deal with it cracked part of me open and that smile spilled out.

I opened my eyes.

This was awesome. When did it get awesome? Was I holding onto the desire for his children without realizing it? Had it crept under the covers with me? Had it been in my diet? The air I breathed? When had this glee snuck into my heart?

I pressed my eyes shut against tears. I didn't want to cry. I didn't want my body to have any confusion. The burst of emotion came from a place I didn't know existed. Some string of code in my DNA, some hormonal rush that was more biological than logical.

I was overjoyed. Thrilled to bursting. I jumped up, cleaned myself and still naked, ran to the tablet. I couldn't wait to tell him. The metal and plastic were cold and hard in my hand as I woke the device, and then I stopped.

I wanted to hold him. I wanted his reaction to myself, to own it the way he owned my orgasms. I wanted to feel his strength and his warmth around me when he found out.

Instead of calling him, I made reservations to go home.

When I put the tablet down, I saw the Sharpie on the desk. I picked it up and went to the bathroom and stood in front of the mirror. My body looked the same to me. I turned every which way and saw no difference. His name between my legs was barely visible when I stood, just a few unreadable hashes of black.

I popped the cap off the marker and pressed the tip to the skin below my navel.

"Upside down and backwards," I said to myself. I looked in the mirror. That just confused things.

Right is left and up is down. I drew a J with my right hand, and convinced I was doing it correctly,

coda.

continued until I'd written *Jonathan's baby* across my abdomen.

Then I laughed at myself so hard I lay on the bed and cried with joy.

CHAPTER 26.

MONICA

I couldn't contain myself. It was twenty minutes to boarding and I fidgeted around the terminal wishing I'd taken the gulfstream. I picked up the phone and as much as I wanted to call Jonathan....I just didn't. Not yet. I wanted to see his face and hear his breath. I wanted him to hold me so close I could feel that motherfucking heart beat.

"Mom?"

"Monica, are you all right?" She was wide awake and it was four in the morning in Los Angeles. If I called at noon she would have been sleeping. That was Mom. I'd learned to accept it.

To say my mother's attitude about me changed after I married Jonathan would be a gross understatement. And now she'd be the first person to hear the news from my lips.

"I'm pregnant."

Silence. I didn't realize how quickly I'd been circumnavigating the terminal until I slowed down.

"Mom?" A woman rolled over my foot with her square bag and gave me a dirty look. Fuck her.

"Monya."

"Are you all right?"

"Am I all right? Are you asking if I'm all right? My only daughter marries a dying man in the hospital, nurses him back to health, and gets pregnant with his baby and you ask if I'm all right?"

I started to reply, but she cut me off.

"How can I not be all right? I am so happy I cannot even speak. My God, a baby. A *baby*."

"Thanks, Mom." I was glad I told her, but I didn't feel the explosion of joy I'd hoped for. The

reveal was kind of a let down. It needed to be
Jonathan, but in front of me.

"Where are you? How far along? Do you have
the sickness?"

"I have no idea how long. And I'm not sick at
all. I mean there was a little flu going around, so—"

"Do you have it? You can't catch anything."
Between the worry in her voice, and my flight
number being called, I lost track of the
conversation.

"I know, I know. My plane's boarding. Just,
don't say anything. I haven't told Jonathan yet."

"You can't tell him."

"What? Why?"

"Anything can happen." Her voice took on that
mysterious, awed tone it got when she talked about
the inscrutabilities of God. "You have to wait until
you're twelve weeks. You don't want to disappoint
him."

"Disa—"

I realized what she meant in the middle of the
word. She'd miscarried a few times, and had just
bled the babies away without ever bothering my
father with the gory details. She was who she was.
The fact that I was a different person completely,
healthy young, with every reason to carry a baby to
term didn't matter. She was going to worry about
stuff because that was what she did.

"Okay, Mom. I won't tell." I painted the lie
white and called it a day. "I have to go."

"Call me when you get back."

"Will do."

I walked up to the gate and boarded the plane a
little disconcerted.

I'd dreamed of doing things like flying first class
from New York to LA, booking at the last minute

without a thought to the extra cost. But once I could, I didn't give it a second thought. Taking money for granted seemed to be an unavoidable symptom of actually having money.

I got the window, and leaned my head into it as soon as I sat. I watched New York get as small as a Lego set, with pieces scattered around the outer boroughs and stacked beautifully on the erection-shaped island in the middle. The evening air was crystal clear, even on a weekday. I'd been shocked at how little pollution there was, and as we flew away, chasing the setting sun, I prepared my self for the soup-thick air of my home.

Should we bring up a baby there? Los Angeles, with all of its silicone reality and blind eyes to real problems? The poverty we swept under the rug, the crumbling school system, the undercurrent of violence and ferocity, coexisted with my little hipster world, and was completely foreign to Jonathan's. Should we go somewhere cleaner? More real? More wholesome? More sincere?

I didn't even know what I wanted from having children. I didn't know what questions to ask. I needed Jonathan to even continue thinking about it. Past his excitement, the happiness I knew my news would inspire, he'd have ideas. I wanted to hear them, all of them. I wanted to hear his dreams for the future and I wanted him to talk far ahead. Ten years. Twenty. Thirty, even. Because I was having his baby, and god damnit, by hook or crook, he was going to live.

CHAPTER 27.

JONATHAN

Petra stood in front of my plane in her uniform, carrying a navy blue bundle of blankets in her arms. Both my pilots were complete professionals, but Petra made most professionals look like part-timers. Jacques stood next to her, also in uniform, but tired, as if he was he one who had been nursing a newborn.

"You flying?" I said to him after Lil let me out of the car and handed me my bag. "You look too tired to drive. Can Lil give you a lift?"

"He'll take you up on that," Petra said with a smile as she handed me the bundle she carried.

"Claude," I said as I took him in my arms. He still had the squishy pink look of a newborn. He looked angelic in the mid morning light. "Nice-looking kid, Jacques. Lucky thing your wife has strong genes."

Petra pressed her lips together as if she was trying not to smile. "If he roots, come and get me."

"Roots?" Claude waved his hands around, not knowing what they were for or if they were even his. I gave him my finger and he clutched it.

"Tries to latch onto your breast."

"Ah. I'm sure I have a bad joke somewhere, but it flew out of my head."

"That happens." Jacques picked up my bag. "I'll help you up. Lange's gonna copilot. He's running through the terminal as we speak."

"I owe you for this." Worse than owing him, having that baby in my arms made me feel like a petulant, spoiled ass who couldn't wait a day to see his wife.

Jacques shrugged. "You're usually pretty easy. And you know, it's nice to see you getting around again."

I would have questioned him on how obvious it was to everyone that I wasn't myself, but it didn't matter. The baby wiped it all away. I picked a piece of crud from his eye, and when I pulled my arms back, Petra had put the diaper bag around my shoulder.

"He needs to be changed fifteen minutes after a feeding, which, I nursed him in the car, so you'd better get to it. You know how to change a diaper?"

"I did it for my nephew once."

"Great. If he cries you swaddle him tight. I'll show you how. He doesn't use a pacifier, but you might let him suck on your finger for a minute when he's wrapped. And you hold him and bounce him. Not much rocking, just bouncing. The noise of the plane will probably put him to sleep, but if not he'll scream. That's on you, sir. I can't come out of the cockpit for fussy. Only hungry."

"Were you saying something? I was distracted."

I smiled at her to let her know I was kidding. "We have half an hour or so of flight prep. If you play your cards right, he'll sleep through it."

Jacques started up the stairs, and indicated I should follow.

This was going to be the longest flight of my life, and I was ready for it.

CHAPTER 28.

MONICA

I slept a little, all wrapped in my first-class-approved blanket. I woke close to landing at the same time of day as I left, chasing the sky from blue-to-yellow. The city below was grey, blanketed in a thick brown smog, and we were descending right into it.

I hadn't been dreaming, but when I woke, it was mid question. What would it be like to be pregnant? Would I be sick? Active? What could I eat? Could I fly? Could I fuck? I didn't even have a doctor, really. I'd run to the clinic for my last depo shot, just because it was more convenient. No way I could do that for this pregnancy. Jonathan wouldn't allow it and I didn't want to. I wanted the best, even if I didn't know what that meant yet.

I hustled through baggage and to a taxi stand. If I knew Jonathan, he'd be in bed, still, but I wasn't going to make it home before his run. I sat in the back of the cab, tapping my fingers, wondering how much of a surprise I wanted to deliver. I'd snuck back without using any of his staff, so he had no way of knowing I was home. It could be too much of a surprise. Not quite thirty people jumping out from behind the couch and yelling "Happy Birthday!" but not a soothing welcome home either.

I turned my phone on. I could call him. But what if he came hoe from his run, and I was just there in a total non-shocking kind of way? Then I could tell him. I ran alternate scenarios through my head. In the bed, naked. In the kitchen, making eggs. I could write him a note and leave it on the banister. I could call first and tell him to wait

151

somewhere in the house. I considered everything as the cab slid onto the 105 freeway toward home.

CHAPTER 29.

JONATHAN

I'd gotten the baby to sleep without much trouble. He sucked on my finger and I sang him a few off-key verses of *Collared*. Thankfully, Petra couldn't hear me give her son evil ideas, and he couldn't understand a word of it as his age. They only spoke French to him anyway.

The plane started down the runway. I put my feet on the seat across from me and slipped my phone out. I wanted everything to be perfect when I landed. I needed to know where she was, who she'd be with, and how close she was going to be to the hotel.

"Quentin?" I said when he answered. He was somewhere loud, a club or restaurant, and I couldn't yell with a sleeping baby in my arms. I just hung up and texted him.

—Is Monica with you?—

—I have no idea where she's off to—

—You were supposed to watch her—

—Sorry, man. Didn't work out that way. Haven't seen her since last night. The sessions broke down. Starting up again on Tuesday—

Damnit. I couldn't hold Quentin responsible, and that was the problem. He was a musician and he owed me nothing, and now Monica was MIA. How did I know she wasn't being attacked by that singer? Or dead in a ditch? Or getting roofied in some dirtshit club?

I should have hired someone. Should have sent drones to watch her or bugged her purse. I was so busy proving what a nice reasonable guy I was I walked right into this. Fuck that. Never again. I was neither nice nor reasonable when it came to Monica. The next time she went anywhere without me, I was planting a locations chip under her scalp.

I called my wife. She wasn't dead.

"Jonathan? Where are you?"

Would I blow the surprise? I had to think fast.

"I'm on a plane, I'll be back in a few days. Where are you?"

"No! Oh, Jonathan! I'm home. In the house."

"No!" I immediately looked down at the baby. He was sleeping like a doll. "Don't move!" I said, then hung up.

"Petra!" I called from the seat. That wasn't going to work, and it was going to wake the baby. I reached for the intercom. Couldn't get it. Shifted. The plane sped up. It was going to take off in seconds. I couldn't reach, nor could I put the baby down.

I hit the intercom button with my foot.

"Mister Drazen?" Petra asked. "We're taking off—"

"No. Stop. No take off. I'm going home."

"Oh, *merde!*"

I'd never heard her swear before. It was cute, and I braced myself for what was about to happen, the plane slowed down. I leaned my head back, and Claude rolled his eyes open, then screamed.

The cockpit door clicked open and Petra peeked
out. She was back to her normal level of
professionalism.

"Everything all right?"

"Yeah, I just...don't need to go anymore." I
found myself yelling over the baby. I stood up and
rocked him.

"You need help with Claude?"

"No, I got it. I owe you for stopping the plane."

"My pleasure. I'd rather go home."

"Me too."

CHAPTER 30.

MONICA

I ran to the door when I saw the Bentley across the drive. He got out with a bag, leaving Lil half out of the car when he said something to her with a wave of his hand. She got back in and drove out.

He turned to the door, jacket under his arm and bag over his shoulder. His hair was a little disheveled and his cheeks were scrubby with two days of beard. His shirt was open to the second button, and his sleeves were rolled to the elbow, revealing his taut forearms and strong wrists. And his hands. Those hands. Like the marble statue of David, an altar to the aesthetics of perfect proportions.

"Hi," I said as he strode to me.

"What's this about?" He looked stern, but under it, he was pleased to see me.

"You were supposed to be home."

"I was. But let's cut the supposed to's. If you came home to get laid you shouldn't be wearing clothes. So let's fix that."

He reached for me, just touching the red scarf around my neck, but I backed up.

"I want to try something different."

"Really?" He stepped forward again. One more step and we'd be in the house.

"I want you to do what I tell you," I said. He stepped forward again. I backed up, and we were inside.

"Like how?" He slammed the door shut.

"Like I'm in charge."

He dropped his bag and jacket with a thud. "I told you I don't bottom." His arm shot out and grabbed me by the waist.

I pushed him away. "Today, I'm the boss."

"You want to start a limits list? We won't get laid for a month."

"You have to just trust me." I pushed him backward and he fell into a chair.

"Monica," his voice got serious. "Really. This is not going to work."

I put my hands on the arms of the chair and leaned on them until my nose was an inch from his.

"You smell like baby powder."

"And you smell like you want to piss me off."

"Trust me." I placed his hand on the arms of the chair, laying them flat. "I won't tie you up or hurt you. That's mine. But I want you to stay still. That's all."

I pulled my scarf off.

"Better watch it with that thing," he said. "I know how to use it."

I got behind him and tied it around his eyes.

"Monica?"

"Jonathan?"

"I'm not turned on."

"You will be."

I peeled my clothes off quickly. I'd showered but with no effort taken to scrub off the sharpie, I was still marked with his name and the location of his baby. I took a deep breath. He tapped his finger, mouth set in a tight line. Not turned on. Almost frightening in his stress. He really didn't like taking orders. But he was going to love this. I turned my naked back to him, toward the Mondrian over the fireplace, and crossed my arms over my abdomen. I didn't know how long I was going to last. I felt like a bottle of soda someone had shaken, but left sealed.

"Take the blindfold off," I said.

I heard a rustle behind me.

"You have a great ass."

I turned, fully nude before him, and after half a second, moved my arms to my side. His eyes worked their way from my face, to my tits, hardening them without even touching them, down my body until he stopped where I'd written *Jonathan's baby*.

"Really?" he said.

"Really."

He laughed. Not a laugh of humor or derision, just delight. Pure, childlike delight. I had to laugh with him. I got on my knees and crawled to him, still laughing, and he kissed me all over, my cheeks, my forehead, my neck. His hands went everywhere, as if touching all the parts he loved, then he kissed my mouth, long hard and deep.

"Thank you," he said, breaking the kiss for half a second before putting his lips on me again..

"No problem." It was the least I could say, a joke of miniature proportions.

"You know you wrote it backwards, right?" I leaned back and looked at my abdomen. Is it because you have your doubts?"

"No. I did it in the mirror."

He pushed against me until my back was on the wool rug, and he was over me like an unclouded sky.

"Are you happy?" he asked.

I put my hands on his cheeks. "I didn't think I would be. But, I don't know. I'm just elated. I feel like I'm walking on air."

He put my hands over my head and kissed me. "I want to say thank you over and over. I find myself at a loss for words otherwise."

"Don't speak. Just fuck me."

"I want you, I love you, you're mine." He said it all in a string, as if it was one thought. "Do we need a bigger house?"

"This is plenty of space."

"We have to ask Sheila what schools to apply to."

"We can worry about that later."

"The wait lists for preschool are four years long."

"That's obscene."

"I have to set up a trust and fund it. Tomorrow, I'll call Margie and have it done."

My face wasn't supposed to tighten, but I feared it did, so I just spoke my mind. "The Swiss thing. You need to promise me you're going to fund that. Before the trusts."

"The trust is easier."

"I don't care if the kid grows up poor. I care that it has a father."

"Hope is deadly."

"Maybe. But tell me you don't have a little bit now? Or some reason to hope you're not taking a bunch of pills so you can fuck me harder and more often? Don't you want to try? I mean, look. Think of it this way. Maybe you'll save someone else."

"Monica. You don't know what this does to me. The idea of leaving you alone. I've been, I think, afraid to make you happy because of what we both know is coming."

I brushed my finger across the scruff on his cheek, this living man, blood beating through him as he scratched an clawed to be reasonable, sensible, and mature while still living life corner to corner. I'd thought I understood his struggle, but I didn't. I thought he just wanted to live or die. I thought he just wanted to be in the moment and not worry, but he'd carried the weight of his own life alongside the weight of mine.

"All I want is for you to try," I said. "Let me and the baby know we're worth you fighting for your life."

He smiled ruefully. "You make compelling arguments. When we met, I thought you were studying law."

"Because I threatened to sue you?"

"It was cute. And you were so sexy, the way you tried to back me into a corner. I wanted to bend you over that desk and spank you raw. The minute I laid eyes on you, I wanted to fuck you until you begged."

"Do it now."

He kissed the space between my breasts. "You came when you weren't supposed to. I had plans, I don't think I can follow through on them."

"Don't you dare."

He put his ear between *Jonathan's* and *baby*. "I can't hear anything. When is he coming?"

"She's coming in late January. And I'm coming today. I'm still me. Do everything. Don't make me beg. Or make me beg. Whichever. Just make me."

He got on his knees and pulled my legs apart until his name was visible, looking at me everywhere as if searching for something inside himself, bathing me in the scalding water of his gaze.

He smirked and put his eyes on mine. "I'm thinking. Can I destroy you when you're carrying my baby?"

"Yes, you can."

He slapped the inside of my thigh. It stung like hell because it was unexpected. I gasped and bit my lip. "I'll decide what I can and can't do. And I'll decide what you can do. Do you understand?"

"Hurt me," I whispered.

He slapped the inside of my other thigh, and yes, it hurt. And yes it was demeaning and yes I pulled away. I thought I might come from that alone.

"No more demands, Goddess. I have ways to hurt you that aren't as much fun." He pulled the red scarf off the arm of the chair. "No talking. No whimpering. No crying. Not a peep out of you. Just yes and no."

"Yes." I couldn't imagine, as he kneeled above me, his knees keeping mine apart, that the word *no* would exit my lips.

"Put your hands over your head and grab the table leg."

I did it, stretching to reach the leg of the heavy sideboard.

"I haven't tied you up since the surgery. You've noticed?"

"Yes."

He leaned over me and wrapped the scarf around my wrists, attaching it to the sideboard as he spoke. "I was nervous. I kept dreaming the heart would leave me. Probably all the talk of rejection going to my head. But I had a worry that it would happen while you were tied up, and you'd be trapped until someone came." He leaned back and checked his work by pulling me toward him, until my arms were completely extended. "I know it wasn't sensible. But it was there." He stood up and reached for something in the bag he was about to take on the plane. His blue book. "You got away with a lot in the meantime."

"Yes," I said.

"Open your mouth." I did, and he put the book in it. "Hold this for me."

I bit down on the leather. He stepped back, and the book blocked my view of him. I heard the clink of his belt and the rustle of clothes, but I couldn't see him. I could only see the damn book.

"The rules, and you can tell me what you object to when I take the book out of your mouth…the rules are this. I'm going to do what I want to your body. You're going to have your safewords. If you worry about the baby for one second, you use them. And if I worry, I'm stopping the scene. It doesn't matter if those worries make sense. And when you start showing, we're renegotiating."

He pulled my legs up and bent my knees until my ass was up off the rug, then he took the book out of my mouth. He was naked and perfect from his scar to his huge cock. Lithe and strong. Nimble and taut.

"Yes or no, Monica." He slapped the book on his palm.

"Yes, sir."

"Good." The book landed on my ass with a *thwack*. I chirped and held my cry. He paused, then smacked me again. Paused, letting me feel the delicious sting. "Yesterday. You forgot that I own your orgasms. That means, I say how and when you come." *Thwack*. "Every time." *Thwack*.

"Sorry."

"You don't sound sorry."

"I'm not."

"You were getting three. Now you're getting four for lying. Count with me."

The book landed between my legs, flat on my engorged clit, and I bit back a scream. It hurt, stung, burned in the opening notes, and the echo was pure pleasure.

"How many is that?" he asked.

"One."

He smacked it again, and I twisted away at the same time as I wanted it again. He straightened me and spread my legs exposing me to him.

"Count."

"Two."

"You okay?"

"Yes."

Thwap. Harder than the others. I held back a scream.

"Breathe," he demanded.

"Three!"

"Last one."

He did it again, and it hurt bad, but it left a rush of warm pre-orgasm quiver in its wake. How had I ever lived without this? How had I ever had an orgasm without the counterpoint of pain?

"Four," I said through my teeth. He put the book aside and slid his fingers in me.

"You're soaked." He draw his wet fingers over my clit, and it burned, and that burn, not his touch on me, nearly put me over the edge into orgasm. "And you're close. What am I going to do with you?"

Begging him to fuck me might cause an indefinite delay where I was told to think about what it meant to make demands out of turn, so I said nothing. He moved his hand over me, setting my soreness on fire.

He leaned over me and slid his dick into me. I gasped from the pain, and the rawness which had brought every nerve ending into his alert. I was sensitive at every range of the spectrum, and stretching me open, putting his whole length into me, I strained against the ties from the pain and the pleasure.

I expected him to take me like an animal. But he didn't he shifted slowly, making sure I felt every inch. He pushed against my clit, angling himself so he rubbed against it, slowly, slowly, in a tortuous rhythm.

"Please," I whispered.

"You wanted something?"

"Faster."

He didn't go faster. If I'd had a metronome to count by, my bet would be on slower.

"Why?" he asked.

"I want to come."

"Really?"

"Please."

He pressed into me, breathing the words into my cheek. "You are so good. But you have to wait."

"I can't."

"Do you know what happens when you rush? Things don't go right. They're not full. Not complete. If I let you come now, you'll be conscious. You'll say thank you and start thinking about music before you even close your legs." He pulled out slowly, and pushed back in. I moved my hips into him to speed it up, but he adjusted and made it worse. I groaned.

"If I let you come now," he continued, "you'll be satisfied. But you deserve better than that. You deserve to have your mind erased."

"I have a snappy comeback. But I can't breathe."

He moved as if we were underwater. The pressure built, and stayed, and built again, never breaking. What should have taken a second, took several. My brain told me I was coming, but I didn't and I stayed in the netherworld between knowing I was going to come, and actually doing it. The

ultimate mix of pain and pleasure. A tug of war
between two matched opponents.

CHAPTER 31.

JONATHAN

If I told her to add two and two, I don't think she could have answered. It did occur to me to ask for a little simple math, but we were treading a wire-thin path as it was. If I pulled her back too far, I'd confuse her body and ruin the orgasm. She wouldn't be able to have a good one until her body came down fully and her over stimulated nerves recovered, which could take hours. That was never fun. It made everyone cranky.

But I wanted to see how far I could go, and how much pain this caused, because there was going to be a time, soon, when the bruises and contusions weren't going to wash, and I was going to derive no pleasure from hurting her. It was one thing to break and push a consenting adult. It was another to spank and grab a pregnant woman until she was black-and-blue. I had to find other ways to dominate her or we were both going to wind up unsatisfied and discontented. Controlling her orgasms to the point of pain was a possibility. She was suffering, and she loved it almost as much as I did.

She was giving herself to me in that microcosm of her pleasure, and especially her pain, because in the macrocosm of her love she was giving me what I wanted most, a family, a home, roots that were mine completely. Nothing borrowed. Nothing temporary. Through all her doubts and legitimate fears, she was taking a leap of faith into the net of my happiness.

I was going to live for her, for the family she was about to give me, for the home she agreed to create. My orbit around her was going to get tighter and tighter until, for better or worse, we fused into a single sun.

A tear dropped from the corner of her left eye, and I kissed it, still shifting with a slow, grinding rhythm. I was going to have to pull her over the edge. It was the perfect time. Another second would be too late.

I gave her no permission to come, but got up on my knees and thrust deep and hard. Her eyes opened wide, and rolled back with the second thrust.

I had complete control over her.

What that did for me, there were no words. Just a peace. A sloughing off of life and its pressures and worries. I existed only in this corner of the world, and it was mine, fully under my purview. The rush of euphoria that followed was submission in itself, to the act, to her, to the power she'd given me.

"May I come?" she whimpered.

"Yes."

I took her. Made her mine. I saw the tide coming in her and encouraged it. When she was midway, I'd slow down to make it last, then I'd let go and fill her with me.

It was a good plan. But I looked down as she started to cry my name.

I don't know what I was looking for. Maybe I wanted to see our connection point when I came, or see her cunt pulsing around me. But that's not what I saw.

I shriveled up. Stopped moving.

My name, ringing in my ears as I looked at my dick, seeing something horrifying, like a death of joy, and I couldn't hear my name any more. Maybe she was screaming in her orgasm, or in pain, or blame, I didn't know, but I couldn't form a sentence or command.

The streak of blood on my dick was unmistakable.

I only had one word in my head.

"Tangerine."

CHAPTER 32.

MONICA

"What?"

I was pulled so far out of my orgasm my body went rigid and my mind was soaked in adrenaline. He might as well have screamed *Stop* in my ear. I yanked my hands against the ties with a motion so violent I could hear stuff clatter and clunk as it fell.

His cock was streaked in red. It wasn't supposed to be. Not unless something was broken. And we weren't doing broken. We were doing celebration. This was wrong. Everything was wrong. I pulled again, even as he reached up to het the scarf undone.

"Monica! Stay still. Give me a second."

But all my yanking and pulling had tightened the knot, and he growled as he tried to pick it loose and failed.

"Say it's from hitting me. Please say it's from—"

"I don't know what it's from. Just stay still."

I couldn't. I had no control over my body. I yanked and pulled, trying to slip free, but my husband knew knots like he knew ice cubes and sore bottoms, and if he'd set up the knot to keep me from slipping out, I wasn't slipping out.

"Jonathan," I said without a plan to say a thing after. Him, I just wanted him. I wanted to say his name to gather strength. He got up, and I had full view of his beautiful, bloodied cock.

"Don't leave me."

"I'm not." He walked away.

"Don't leave me here!"

But he did. He walked away, and I don't know why I felt so bereft. Some need to run away, coupled with the inability to even lower my arms made me panic, because I could feel something dripping down my leg. And he wasn't there. He was going to the fucking kitchen, and then I heard knives clack and his footsteps back toward me I calmed. Barely.

He came back the a bread knife and leaned over my hands.

"Stay still," he said. "Please. I don't want to cut you."

He put the knife to the scarf. "What's happening?" I asked.

"I don't know." His concentration stayed on my bound wrists.

"I don't want to lose it."

"Me neither."

"It's from spanking me. That's all. You hurt me worse than I thought. Let's not do that again, okay?"

"Sure." He laid his hands on my wrists, pressing them apart and making the fabric between them taut as he sliced the scarf open with a *snap*.

I got my arms under me and started to get up, but Jonathan pushed me down. I resisted. He pushed harder.

"Hold on. Gravity."

"That doesn't even make sense."

"I know, I know."

He put his arms under my shoulders and my knees and carried me to the couch. I was sore where he'd hit me, and that was the reason for the blood, but he seemed worried, and I wanted to respect that. I didn't want to be dismissive or call him silly, but his knotted brow and the taut line of his jaw made me want to stroke away his fear.

He leaned over me and caressed my cheeks. "Can you wait here while I get dressed and get you some clothes?"

"Why?"

He got up and plucked his clothes off the floor. "We're going to the hospital."

I got my elbows under me to sit up and with only one arm in his shirt, he rushed to push me down. "It's nothing, Jonathan. I'm sure of it." I said it to calm him, but I wasn't sure if I believed it out of anything but necessity.

"Then humor me. Lie back." I did, and when he saw I'd done it, he trotted upstairs. I looked down at his name inside my thighs. I was drawn on like a cinderblock wall in gangland, Jonathan's dominion over me in black sharpie, his territory marked in permanent ink.

Was I losing the baby? And so what if I was? What was the big deal? I didn't even want to have children right now. I wanted nothing to do with it. Jonathan was going to die before the kid was in high school after a tortuous wait for a second heart. What kind of selfish bitch creates a child to go through that?

All I had to do was go back to the me of a few days ago. Nothing had changed.

Except everything. Except having carried that baby knowingly for two days, I'd had a cellular alchemy. The shape of my brain and my heart had shifted, grown. I wasn't the same person. I wanted that baby. I wanted it so bad, and I didn't even know it.

I wanted this to be nothing. An embarrassing symptom of rough sex play, but the twitch in my abdomen, the tightness told me otherwise.

Jonathan came down the stairs dressed, with a dress over his arm.

"Do you think they can save it?" I asked, my voice breaking on "save."

"I don't know." He sat on the edge of the couch. "Arms up."

I raised my arms and he put the long, modest dress over me. He snapped out a pair of simple cotton underwear and slipped them over my ankles, drew them up my legs and over me.

"I was supposed to get rid of all that underwear," I said.

"Sometimes you need it." He stood aside the couch. I heard the crunch of tires on pebbles outside. "Is it Lil?"

"Yes. I texted her." He put his arms under me and picked my up, carrying me toward the door. "I don't think I can drive."

"Thank God for her."

I looped my arms around his neck and he carried me out.

"Sir." Lil said as she opened the back door. "Mrs. Drazen, I hope you're all right."

"I'm sure it's nothing."

I don't know why I said that. As the minutes passed I started to think that was some whitewash of hope on a steaming pile of tragedy.

Jonathan held me tight and somehow, got me in without putting me down. I shifted down and put my head on his lap. Lil looked into the back.

"Sequoia?" she asked.

"Yes."

"No!" I said, rigid. I looked up at Jonathan. "No. Anywhere but there. Please. I can't."

"It's the best obstetrics unit in the world, Monica."

"I don't care. I can't go back there. I can't. Let's go to Hollywood Methodist."

"It's a different ward entirely."

"Do you know how far out of my way I go to not drive past it? And it's on Beverly, so yeah, I'd rather be late than see it. I'd rather go to the urgent care clinic on Sunset. I'd rather see the witch doctor in Silver Lake than go anywhere near that hospital. It smells like death. It's hell. Nine stories of fucking hell, and I won't go."

Jonathan looked down at me for a second, then back to Lil. "Drive."

"Jonathan!" I said as Lil closed the door. I tried to get up but he pulled me down.

"Listen to me," he said. "I know how you feel. Believe me. I get it. But that was enough blood to scare the hell out of me, and it wasn't enough to convince me this is completely over. And if we lose this baby because we went to a second rate hospital or nowhere at all, because we were scared…Well, I'd like to know how you're going to forgive yourself. Because you're going to have to teach me."

I looked away from him. His gaze was going to break me. It was a wall of resolve. He was doing what he wanted to do and I had to go along.

From my angle on his lap, all I could see was the grey blue glass of the sky, streetlights and telephone poles zipping by. A speck of bird or plane.

He was right.

Fear was fungible and death was forever. Overcome one to face the other. Blah blah. I didn't want to be right. I wanted to fall down a fall down a hole of despair or climb a pillar of hope, and reason and rationality were distractions from the choice.

Reaching up for the hope, I touched his face. "I'm sure it's fine. We're just overreacting."

"I hope so."

"Didn't Jessica miscarry? What happened?"

He turned to the window. "We were throwing an event at the house. Some fundraiser for the artist co-op she was in. She just takes my hand and brings me into the house. Doesn't break a beat, and I'm following her and I can see the blood inside her stockings. I picked her up and carried her to the car, but it was too late. It was a mess before we even got there. So much blood. I never saw her cry except in the front seat of my car. The pain was so bad, and you know, I asked her how long it hurt before she told me."

He stopped without answering.

"Could they have saved it?"

"The doctor wouldn't guarantee anything, but just said, next time we should come right away."

I relaxed into that, watching the fancy streetlights of Santa Monica turn into the more urban, less fussy designs of the west side of LA.

"I had pain yesterday but I thought I had the flu."

"Let's see what happens."

"If we lose it, do we try again?"

"I don't know."

That didn't help. If he pulled back from taking what he wanted most, what he'd *always* wanted most, then I didn't know who he was any more.

"Did you try again with Jessica?" I flinched from my own question. It sounded petty and mean. The situations couldn't have been more different. But I wanted to know what to expect from him. Did he give up or truck on?

If he heard the question as cutting, he didn't
show it. "We both got checked out. I was fine, but
her uterus had a shape that made it hard for her to
go to term. And we were fine, but it never took
again. In a way it improved things between us for
awhile."

I cupped his face in my hands, and he looked
back down at me, then leaned over and kissed me.
"This won't end us," he said. "I swear if it's the last
thing I do, I'm keeping you."

The car stopped.

"I'm ready," I said. "If you stay by me. I'm
ready."

Lil opened the door, and Jonathan carried me
through the sliding glass doors into Sequoia
Hospital. Hell on earth. I closed my eyes, but the
smell was still there, and the ambient noise, and
when something somewhere beeped, I clung to him.

CHAPTER 33.

JONATHAN

I'd called ahead while gathering our clothes, and was able to carry her right up to the second floor. We were offered a gurney right outside the elevator, and I put her on it, insisting even when she clutched me. She weighed nothing to me. I could have carried her ten more miles, but I knew hospitals better than I wanted to, and she needed to be on the gurney.

We exited onto the maternity ward. The first thing I heard was people laughing, and I shot a look down to Monica to see if she heard it. I thought it would relax her. Maternity wards were gentle places with better results than the parts of the hospital she'd been stuck in for weeks.

Her eyes were clamped shut, as if she was a child who didn't want to see anything scary. I was about to make some wisecrack about ocean views and a full buffet. Describe the dancing girls and rare art she was missing. Anything to calm her down. A chuckle. Even if she slapped me and told me to shut up, it would have been preferable to seeing her coiled in dread.

"Mister Drazen," the young woman in the blue scrubs said. It had taken Dr. Solis seconds to recommend this young woman with the flat brown ponytail above all others.

"Are you Dr. Blakely?"

"Yes. Dr. Solis told me you'd be coming." She looked at Monica. "How are you feeling?"

"Fine," my wife lied.

"This way, then."

The nurse, a muscular woman in his forties in a military cut, asked a battery of stupid questions. Monnica answered them with her eyes closed.

"Mister Drazen," Blakely said as she stepped into the exam room in front of the gurney. "Dr. Solis says you're immunosuppressed?"

"Yes?"

"You shouldn't be in a hospital."

Monica opened her eyes. "Go," she said.

"I'll text you our findings," Blakely said as they moved Monica from gurney to table. She seemed so helpless, so separate from her mind and will, so corporeal as she stretched across, and her dress hitched above her knees, and I saw the sharpie script of *Jo* and *erty*.

I was not abdicating responsibility. Not the medical part. I knew my limitations. But I wasn't turning my back on her and I wasn't letting her sit, alone and hurt, while I protected my immune system.

"I'll stay, thank you."

"Jonathan, please," Monica said. "She's right. I'll be ok if you keep your phone on. Really, I'm not freaked out. You need to go."

But she was freaked out. From the ends of her hair, through the writing on her thighs to the tips of her toenails she was terrified. I hadn't known her that long, and I had plenty to learn about her. But I knew god damn well when she was lying about her comfort to protect me. We'd both done that enough to get PhD's in it.

"I'm not going," I said, then turned to Dr. Blakely. "This is my wife, and she needs me. I don't want to hear, from either of you, that I should go home and live in a bubble and wait for a fucking text telling me what's happening with my family."

I sat in the seat next to the table and held her hand.

"He can wear a mask outside maternity," the nurse suggested as she tapped on a computer keyboard.

"Will you?" asked Monica.

"Fine."

Dr. Blakely sat down on a stool at the end of the table. "You're not my patient," she said. "Dr. Solis will have what to say. Let's get these underpants off."

Monica picked up her butt and the doctor helped her slide out of them. The nurse started to pick up her dress, but glanced at me once she saw the words *Jonathan's Property*. I wanted to mention it, or make a tension-splitting joke, but I didn't want to embarrass Monica. The nurse put crinkled paper that draped from the waist down. The doctor spread her legs and I thanked God Solis had recommended a woman.

"Well, no question of paternity," she said, looking over the paper. "The baby has to work on his handwriting, though."

The joke wasn't that good, but I was glad she made it, because the tension fell off my wife as she laughed.

"All right," the doctor smiled behind her mask, "let's see what we have here." Monica cringed and I heard a squishing noise. I held her hand.

"Plug is in place."

More tension dropped off Monica. Maybe she was right. Maybe the book was the wrong tool. Maybe I was going to have to start getting proper toys. I was going to have to stop using whatever was on hand if it was going to make her bleed.

The doctor put the sheet back and put her Monica's legs down. The nurse wheeled a cart over to the table.

"I'm supposed to tell you jokes," I said. "Something clever and funny to take the edge off."

Blakely and the nurse said things I didn't understand and they exposed Monica's abdomen. So much like my own experience as a patient. Experts talking about me as if I wasn't there, huddling together before approaching with an approved line of bullshit.

Blakely squeezed clear gel on her abdomen as if every patient had the baby's ownership scrawled backwards on the mother.

"I'm waiting," Monica said. "I know you have a few thousand jokes in there."

"Knock knock."

She laughed, as if that was the whole entire joke, which it was. I didn't know any knock knock jokes.

The screen went live, as if it had been fingerpainted in shades of grey. We both watched as if it was the seventh game of the world series, with no idea of what we were seeing.

Silence. And too long. Shouldn't we be hearing a heartbeat? I'd had sonograms when I was in the hospital and I always heard whooshing.

I squeezed her hand. The doctor slid the wand over her abdomen, tapping keys.

"Okay," Dr. Blakely said. "Well, that explains it." She pointed to a black oval. "This is the ovum, and typically we have a little peanut-sized blur in there, and there isn't. It's empty."

"What does that mean?" Monica asked.

"Well, it's a blighted ovum. Meaning, the egg was fertilized, and made it to the uterus, but the cells stopped dividing. Either the cells were reproducing incorrectly, or there was some other technical malfunction. Your body kept doing it's

179

job, though. And so you have an ovum and the beginnings of a placenta." Blakely shut the machine.

Monica went white, and something in me did too. I wanted to throttle this young doctor. I wanted to choke her until she admitted she was wrong, she'd misread the images. It was all a big mistake and there was a baby in there, right as rain, thriving.

"I was travelling," Monica said. "Did that do it?"

"Probably not."

"We're rough in bed, the two of us." Monica was past sense. Her hand had gone cold and she was babbling. "I shouldn't say this but you're a doctor right? I mean, sometimes, it's just, well like I said we get rough and—"

"I saw the bruising, and no. That wouldn't cause this. I'm sorry. The good news is, you're in perfect shape. You should be able to conceive again without a problem."

I stood up. "Thank you, Doctor." I held out my hand. These people had to leave immediately. I got it. I heard it. I needed to be alone with my wife.

"Not so fast. Let me give you a quick rundown, then I'll leave you alone. You have tissue in your uterus your body needs to get rid off. It's messy and painful, and it could start today or next week. Most patients opt for us to remove it by dilating the cervix and scraping the uterus. That shortens the—"

"No," Monica pointing her chin up. "I'm not evicting the baby."

"Mrs. Drazen, I'm sorry, but there is no baby."

"Don't you tell me there's no baby!"

She was pure kinetic energy. A blur. Her limbs were still, but poised to shake the earth free of its orbit. I put myself between the two women.

"There is a motherfucking baby!" Monica called from behind me. I felt the same as she did. I felt all her anger and denial, but I couldn't allow myself to get lost in it.

"Is there anything else, Doctor?" I asked. She had to get out before we were escorted out.

Unfazed by Monica's denials, she took a card out of her pocket. "Call me if the pain is really bad. I'll prescribe something."

"Pain?" Monica's voice shot from behind me. "I can take pain. Just try me."

I took the card. This was it. So much had changed in the past four hours, I felt numb. I hadn't even had a chance to process flying to New York, then not flying to New York, then the baby, and the lack of the baby. It had been a day of miserable false starts, ending with the promise of pain for my wife. "Thank you."

"Have her take it easy, if possible. It's going to hurt."

CHAPTER 34.

MONICA

Take it easy. What kind of bullshit was that? How was I supposed to take it easy? Was I supposed to sip pina coladas by the pool and wait for a miscarriage? Like la-di-da let's take a jog and have a good laugh and watch TV and forget that my whole life, everything I thought I wanted changed in the past two days. And now I'm supposed to pretend that didn't happen.

Well, fuck you, Doctor. Fuck you with a big bag of fucking fucks.

Once that fucking fuck of a doctor and her little nurse were gone I flipped them a double bird, because fuck them and fuck this machine and fuck this room and fuck this hospital and fuck the lie I fucking wrote on myself.

"And fuck you," I said to Jonathan when he twirled my underwear on his hand.

"You should get the D&C," he said, looping the cotton panties around my ankles.

"No."

"What if you're in the studio when you start cramping?"

"Fuck the studio. I hate this hospital. I hate everything about it. It's a rat shithole. Everything is beige and pale pink. The decorator should be shot. And they can run fucking potpourri through the vents and it still smells like bleach and death."

He slid my underpants back on, and I let him, because I was too mad, too confused by my tangle of emotions to get dressed and get off the table. Jonathan pulled me into a sitting position.

"Don't fight me," he said, opening the door. His voice was as definitive as ever, telling me my behavior before I had a chance to question it. I didn't know what he meant until he put his arms under me and picked me up, carrying me out the door and down the hall. I put my arms around his neck and rested my head on his shoulder.

"You don't have to look," he said, and I knew what he meant. I closed my eyes and focused on the leather scent of him, pretending bleach and medicine didn't hover around the edges, ignoring the ding of the elevator and the whispering of nurses and doctors in their parallel language. It was so familiar, and so foreign, because though the sounds and smells were the same as the time I spent at my husband's side, I wasn't worried about Jonathan, or even myself. I was just angry, and disappointed, and touching the edges of grieving the loss of something I hadn't even wanted twenty-four hours ago.

"I'm okay," I said into Jonathan's ear as he carried me out of the elevator and across the lobby.

"I know."

"I'm not upset any more."

"I know."

"You can put me down." I opened my eyes. He filled the frame of my vision.

"Nope. You're my wife and I'll carry you where I like."

Lil waited in the roundabout, parked in the red zone as if it was a marker for Bentleys. She opened the back door, and Jonathan poured me in.

I didn't say anything the whole way home. I sat on Jonathan's lap, wrapped in him, head on his shoulder, and somewhere on the 10 freeway, I felt a twinge, and it started.

The doctor had been very explicit about what to expect, and I didn't know if I thought I'd be immune, or I didn't care, or if I simply underestimated what she meant by pain and bleeding.

But by the time Jonathan carried me to the door, I felt as if I'd been stabbed in the stomach.

"Monica?" He swung the door open.

"I think I should go to the bathroom."

"Are you all right?"

"Yeah."

He looked concerned, but let me down, and I ran to the bathroom that was off our bedroom. It had a shower, and a bathtub, and a door that locked. It was a super fancy little corner of the world, and it had a view of the ocean, because what else does a girl need when her body is ridding itself of a blight. Right?

I peeled off my pants and sat on the toilet, hunched in pain so bad, it felt as if my guts were being pulled and tied into a knot at the end of a balloon.

There was a soft rap on the door.

I couldn't do this in front of anyone. Not even him. Not even the man whose chest had been open before me. Not even the one whose bleeding heart I carried every night. I was doing this alone, whatever it was.

I grunted when the air went out of the balloon and the stretching and knotting started again.

"Monica," he said through the door. "I'm calling for pain killers."

"I'm fine!"

Why did I say that? I wasn't fine.

"You were with me in the hospital," he said. "You have a distorted view of pain."

"Don't take this the wrong way," I said, barely able to breathe. "You are the love of my life. But get the fuck away from the door."

"No, I will not leave you." He used his dominant voice and I didn't give a single shit. "Open it."

"*Go jogging!*" I screamed it not because I wanted to scare him, but because the pain intensified by an order of magnitude. I put my head in my hands, and the blood started.

CHAPTER 35.

JONATHAN

The door was locked. Not that I gave a shit on a practical level. A bobby pin could fix that. I could knock the door down or unscrew the knob or hinges. I was sure there was a chainsaw somewhere in the garage. Or hedge clippers. I could have broken that lock with my spit, to be honest. That's how wound up I was. I put my fist to the door for one last threat, but before I pounded it, I heard her hiccup, then sniff, and as badly as that made me want to get into that bathroom, I imagined a sudden bang on the door would only startle her. What would be the point of that?

"I'll tell you what," I said.

No answer. Just breathing.

"I won't break this door down. But I'm staying right here." I sat with my back against the door, forearms on my knees.

She groaned, and I heard her pregnancy ending in a rush. She made an N sound that stretched out like a rubber band.

"Monica?"

"Women have gone through this for centuries, okay? Generations. Just…if you're going to sit at the door like an eavesdropper…"

She stopped, and I could only imagine why. "I'll let you know when I'm through." The last word ended in a squeak. If I broke the door down, I could hold her hand. Or bring her a painkiller. I could be *doing something* instead of sitting against the door imagining what she was going through. I felt trapped and incompetent. I wanted to grab my fitness as a husband back.

That was it. I wasn't leaving her alone.

Bobby pins. I needed just one to open that door. I went to her dresser. The surface was cluttered with a picture of her parents, a crochet runner, a calendar. I opened her nightstand drawer. Old pictures. Sunglasses. Pens. Little notebooks. What the fuck? Where were the bobby pins?

It hit me hard, deflating me. The bobby pins were where they belonged. In the goddamned bathroom.

I stood, by the door, ready to break it down, when I heard her on the other side. She was humming the *Star Spangled Banner* of all things. I put my hands on the door. She groaned the lyrics and I heard a sickening splash.

I couldn't take the door down. I couldn't do that to her, but I couldn't leave her, either.

She was the heart patient and I was the lonely young girl trying to grasp onto anything she could to make something happen. Would I have gone into Paulie Patalano's room to pull the plug? Maybe. Maybe I would have. Because if this kept up for weeks, and was a matter of life and death, yeah, I'd take that door down with a chainsaw even if it scared the shit out of her. I'd take the door down and shove it up someone's ass.

But it only *felt like* life and death. It wasn't. I put my forehead to the door just as she sang "…*and the home of the brave.*"

"Brava," I said.

"Go away," she replied so softly I could barely hear her through the door.

"Is America the Beautiful next?"

"Not until the seventh inning."

"I'll wait out here all day."

"I wanted this baby, Jonathan. Once I found out, I did. But before that…Do you think not wanting it…it's so stupid."

"You didn't miscarry because you didn't want it. You didn't scare it away."

"We'll try again. Right?"

She needed that hope. Hope was her power. Her way of coping. She'd do reckless things to keep it alive. She'd murder and betray. She'd be brave and strong, all in the name of hope. If I could take her hope and let it feed me, I might have a nourished life, no matter its length.

"Yes, Monica. We can try again. Right away. Once you're better."

Another groan, and she started the *Star Spangled Banner* again.

I put my hands on the door as if that was soothing at all to the woman on the other side. The song passed, and silence followed, interrupted by a few sniffs, a few breaths, a few hummed bars of something I couldn't identify. I sat at the door and listened. I didn't know how else to care for her but to make that door into my love, touching the wood as if it was skin, comforting her through it, making her safe with space and matter between us. I didn't know how much time passed before she spoke.

"Are you there?"

"Yes."

"I can't flush. I just….I can't."

"Do you want me to do it?"

A long pause followed.

CHAPTER 36.

MONICA

This was ridiculous. Everything about it. Me on the toilet for over an hour, cramping like it was my job. The crime scene-worthy mess. My compassionate and gorgeous husband standing outside, asking me if I'd like him to flush the baby.

I should just do it. Then I could run into the shower, do a quick clean up of the floor and outside of the bowl, exit looking fresh. I knew this would continue for a few days, but not like this. Not to the point of non-functionality. I felt finished. I felt like the worst was over. I felt empty.

"Monica?"

I couldn't do it. It wasn't a baby. It was tissue that had formed because my body fooled itself into thinking there was a baby, but it was a terminated mission. My uterus just hadn't gotten the memo. So I should just flush instead of being a cliché of a woman who just had a miscarriage.

"I'm unlocking the door," I said. "Just wait until I call you to come in okay?"

"All right."

"And I'm warning you, ahead of time, it's not pretty."

"Consider me warned."

The bathroom was huge, and had a separate bath and shower. Blood dripped on the edges of the toilet from when I'd cramped so badly I moved away from the seat. Otherwise, the room was as pristine as Jonathan's staff could make it.

I unlocked the door and turned the shower on. It was hot in half a second. I don't know how he did that, but money got rid of even the smallest inconveniences of thermodynamics.

189

I stripped, stepped in and clicked the door shut.

The water flowed over my face, scalding hot. I wanted it hotter. Second-degree burn hot. I wanted to sterilize myself from the baby that wasn't a baby. I wanted to forget the feeling of something real, and human dropping from me to its death.

When the water flowed over me fully, a stream of red-stain went down the drain. It was too much. I didn't think I could stand it. I was broken and useless. What had felt real, wasn't. And now I was expect to—

The door clicked open, and Jonathan stood in the shower entrance, fully dressed.

"I'm sorry," I said. "I forgot to call you."

He stepped into the shower, water slapping onto his shirt, sticking it to his skin. Darkening and flattening his hair. He put his arms around me and pressed me to him. His lips brushed my shoulder, and his hands pressed against me, as if he wanted as much of himself touching as much of me as possible.

"I love you," he said.

"I—" A choke made up the rest of the sentence, because I felt lost and empty and he was still there. He was my sky. And through blood and breath, sin and sorrow, I was his sea, and wherever the horizon was, and the world ended, we were there, together.

What had I done to deserve this but fail? Repeatedly and often, I'd failed to deserve him. I'd resisted him, tried to deny him a family, then failed to carry his child.

I wasn't worth him getting his clothes wet, but I needed him. I needed him so badly. To fail for him, and to try again, because having been pregnant for those hours, I couldn't see any future past giving him children.

I clawed at his back and pressed my face to his shoulder. He rocked me under the hot water, sodden and strong, even after my legs couldn't hold me.

"Come on," he said, shutting the shower, "before I flood the floor."

He carried me in his arms for the third time, his feet squishing on the marble tiles. The bath was running and the lights were dimmed. He laid me in the tub.

"I'm sorry," I said.

"For what?" he leaned over the tub, his clothes still soaked, and submerged a sponge. He didn't even roll up his sleeves, he just got them wet.

"For letting the baby go."

"You know I'm not going to accept that apology."

"I feel like I failed you. And hours after getting you all excited. God, I'm such a fuckup."

He put his fingertips to my lips. "Stop."

But it was too late, because my eyes filled up, and the skin behind my face tingled.

"I can't. I can't stop thinking that—" I heaved a breath. "That it's my fault. That I killed it."

He soaped the sponge. "If that were possible, there wouldn't be any unwanted pregnancies."

I was Teflon. Immune to logic, sense, and evidence based reality. I couldn't shake the feeling that I was somehow at fault for this disaster. I couldn't answer him with the straight fact that despite the pure reason of his assertion, I was poisoned. Blighted. My body wasn't fit for a child.

He put the sponge between my thighs and cleaned the last of the blood off. His name was still there and he rubbed until it was gone while I laid my head on the side of the tub and cried.

What shame. Laying in a tub with my legs spread, weeping while my husband scrubbed our baby from between my legs.

But, despite what the scene may have looked like, I wasn't ashamed. I was open, raw, and comforted.

"Thank you," I said. "You're good to me."

He put his hand flat on my abdomen. "You wrote something here too. It's darker." He ran his wet hand over my cheeks, wiping old tears away to make room for the new ones.

"There was a shower in between."

"I'm going to have to work to get it off."

"I don't want to look."

"Don't." He picked up a scrubby thing, tossed it, chose something softer and put soap on it. He was all business for this part of me. I looked at the ceiling as he scrubbed.

"Do you want to hear the last stupid thing that went through my head?" I said.

"If you're willing to hear my stupid thing after."

"I thought, this happened because I wrote it backwards."

"That is stupid."

"What was your stupid thing?" I asked.

"That next time we should tattoo *Jonathan's baby* and it'll stick."

I laughed through my tears. This was Jonathan, a poet in love and a realist in life, thinking superstitious nonsense, just like me.

"Are you cold?" I asked when he put the scrubber down. "Your clothes are soaked."

"I feel trapped in a bag."

"You do look a little vacuum packed."

coda.

He laughed, and I laughed with him. He stood
and peeled off his clothes, getting down to the pure
magnificence of him. I held my arms out and he
stepped into the tub. He leaned his back on me and
I wrapped my legs around his waist.

We laid there until the water got cold.

CHAPTER 37.

EIGHTEEN MONTHS LATER

MONICA

"Today?" Laurelin cried as she zipped my dress. "You agreed to do a show *today*?"

"Tonight, actually." I held up the strapless top with my forearm.

"You're supposed to get swept off your feet to a foreign land." He face was red with irritation, and her fists were tense. She was quite the romantic, our nurse.

"I am. After the show. Two songs in my wedding gown. Darren and I will blow the roof off the place, and then I'll go on my honeymoon."

I kissed her cheek, and when she tried to push me away, I kissed her harder.

"Come on," she said. "Let me get this on you."

Laurelin struggled to get the zipper up, cursing. Her pale blue gown hung on her like a sack, as if its lack of efficiency made it repel off her body. She, Yvonne, and three of Jonathan's sisters were bridesmaids, and they tittered around the waiting room drinking tea and fussing with their makeup.

My hair was braided, of course, and twisted into a bun. Leanne had fashioned a veil of twisted tulle and beadwork, knotted it into the plait and let it fall to the floor. I wasn't into finery, but the dress was gorgeous. Rockstar gorgeous. Underneath it, I had custom made lace garter set with enough hardware and straps to suspend me from the Eiffel tower. I couldn't wait for Jonathan to see it.

I hadn't let him have me in two weeks, which wasn't easy for either of us. But I wanted to be wild with desire on our wedding night, and I wanted to torture him as much as he tortured me.

It was like the weeks after my miscarriage. I couldn't. I was bleeding drop by drop and I felt so raw and hurt I couldn't let him near me. I hated my own skin. Then, one day, as we were getting on the Gulfstream to New York, the rawness left, and I wanted nothing more than his body inside me. He was gentle at first, then once he realized I was all right, he was back to the rough bastard I always knew.

He'd barely left my side since. Where I went, he went. And if he had to travel, I followed him. We brought Laurelin if we had to, and she brought the baby and her husband and kid sometimes.

Jonathan with a baby was magic. He opened up. His sense of humor was turned to silly faces and funny noises. And yet, I couldn't give him one. There was nothing. Not even a threat or a tickle. Just us. And we started talking about adoption, because he only had so long and I wanted joy for him before his heart gave out.

"Any word on Mr. Gevers?" Laurelin asked, as if reading my mind. Andre Gevers was a Dutch man, and the first recipient of an artificial heart made by what we privately called the Swiss Project. Jonathan had funded the research, and though he still promised nothing as far as allowing an artificial heart to be used on him, if it worked I knew he wouldn't say no to a life.

"Stable. The fake heart seems really happy in there."

I held my hand up with fingers crossed so tight I nearly pulled a tendon.

"Two weeks doesn't mean it won't be rejected," Laurelin said. "I'm not trying to be negative, but medical research…there are a lot of failures before something sticks."

"It's going to work. He's going to be an old man."

"Gevers or Jonathan?"

"Yes."

"My brother was born an old man," Margie said, appearing next to me in the mirror wearing a feminine cut tuxedo. She was the best woman. We'd been at a loss for men, so she, Sheila, and Fiona were groomsfolk, along with Eddie, and Darren. "The dress isn't as puff pastry as I feared," she said.

"You look perfectly marriageable yourself."

"That's what I'm told." She handed me the loose bouquet of flowers. "You ready?"

"Thank you, Margie. For everything. I've always felt taken care of with you around."

"My pleasure. Now go."

All my sky blue girls waited at the exit, and I followed them through the stone hallway, into the courtyard. The security detail followed us, as visually conspicuous as they were silent. I didn't know if I'd ever get used to being famous. It had been a year since the EP hit, and seven months since the full album. I was already having daily wrestling matches with my belief that I was a freak and a fraud that Darren and Jonathan had to pull me away from.

And in the middle of the chaos and changing expectations, there was Jonathan, always at my side in public, and always my master and king in private. We'd planned a wedding between plane rides, concerts, family functions, the management of a handful of hotels and enough lovemaking to make my whole life a honeymoon.

Jonathan's divorce made him ineligible for a wedding in a Catholic church. Fortunately,

Episcopalians were less picky, and St. Timothy's was more than happy to do the honors. The church was a huge stone edifice crusted with stained glass and old growth trees in the center of Los Angeles. When I got to the narthex I was overcome with the seriousness of it all. Yes, I'd been married for two years, and yes this was all a big redo for the sake of his family and tradition, but the stones and brass fixtures had seen generations of brides. And the pews, from what I could see, were full of people.

"So much for an intimate event," I mumbled.

"Oh, please Monya," my mother said, "you had no chance of that."

She took my hand in hers and we were hustled to the back of the line.

St. Timothy's had a huge organ, and at the first note, a hush fell over the congregation. I waited at the end of the line with my mother as the bridesmaids and groomsfolk walked down the aisle.

"You ready, Mom?" I asked as Margie and Laurelin went.

"I hoped I wouldn't have to give you away. I hoped I'd meet someone to replace your father."

"No one could replace dad."

The music changed, and I took my mother down the aisle so she could give me away. I was so excited I wanted to run, but my mother took it slow. Too slow.

"Come on, ma."

"You only do this once," she whispered.

I felt like a kid held back from the tree on Christmas morning. I knew what Jonathan looked like. I knew what his tux looked like, how it fit, how the white tie blended with the white shirt and how the line of the sharply-cut black jacket made a perfect triangle from his throat to his waist, like an arrowhead to…well I admit I was thinking of my wedding night.

Cameras had been confiscated. I couldn't look at all the people watching me. I felt their eyes on me. Felt their good wishes.

Once I got halfway down the aisle, I could see Jonathan, because he'd stepped toward the center to see me. Margie tried to pull him back, but it was a wasted effort. Jonathan did what he wanted, when he wanted and how he wanted, and he apparently wanted to watch me rush down the aisle.

Could my heart continue to melt every time I saw him? When would the day come that he had no effect on me? When I took his presence for granted? I couldn't imagine it. He was so straight, so perfect, carrying the formal suit as if it was the most natural thing he could put on his back. The man I'd met had returned, slowly but surely. His sudden visions of his heart rejecting him were gone, and my dreams and fear collapsed under the weight of our intimacy. He was stronger, fitter, more dominant than ever, and he was my perfect life mate.

"Hey," I said when I reached the altar, and he took my hand. "How are you doing? You look nice."

"Nice? I'm surrounded by cross-dressers, and they all look better in a tux than I do."

I put my fingers over my mouth to stifle a laugh. As the congregation sat behind us, Jonathan leaned over and whispered in my ear.

"I own you. I'm going to take a belt to you just because I can."

"Jonathan, we're in church."

He spoke so low I could barely hear him. I shut out the white noise of the church, the ministrations of the bishop, a bellicose man in his sixties and the rustlings of the choir. "This is just a building," Jonathan said. "Worship is later. I'm going to tie your legs over your head with that pretty veil, and I'm going to beat and fuck you so hard the words 'Oh, God,' are going to summon the heavenly host."

His words went right between my legs. We stood together at the altar as people talked about us, as a service was said in our honor. I didn't know if there was a mic somewhere that could pick us up so I turned and spoke directly in his ear, my breath to him, my vocal chords disengaged. A butterfly couldn't hear me.

"I'm singing later. Be gentle with my throat."

His hand twitched. I was expected to know he was aware of all my needs, including my need to sit at a meeting, walk in front of people, or sing. He knew when to be gentle and when to score my skin, because he was inside every part of my life, and any lack of trust warranted a delicious spanking.

"Good thing you don't sing with your ass," he whispered back.

I spit out a nervous laugh that every mic caught and Jonathan's smile broke into a chuckle. The bishop looked back at us, and the congregation stared.

I waved and curtsied.

The bishop looked motioned us front and center.

David held out the red pillow with the rings. They'd been designed as tight coils, like keyrings, to remember our first wedding rings and the circumstances they'd been given under. But they were gold, and they fit right, which would be a nice change.

Jonathan and I positioned ourselves across from each other, and he took the smaller ring. The bishop cleared his throat.

"Mister Drazen, repeat after me. I, Jonathan Drazen—"

"I, Jonathan Drazen,"

"Take thee, Monica Faulkner—"

"Take thee, Monica Faulkner." Jonathan was smiling, the ring hovering over my finger, and I could practically hear the gears in his head turning.

"To be my wedded wife," the bishop said.

"To be my wedded wife," Jonathan said before he turned to the bishop. "You know we memorized this, right?"

"That would be the first time in forty years of officiating weddings."

Laughter floated up from the congregation, and I put my head down to stifle big giggle.

"We thought it was kind of important," Jonathan said.

"Get on with it, then."

"Where were we?"

"Having and holding," the bishop said.

"Thank you," Jonathan squeezed my hand and continued. "…to have and to hold from this day forward, for better for worse, for richer for poorer, in sickness and in health, to love and to cherish, till death us do part." He dropped his voice, as if expressing seriousness, but also to create a web of intimacy around the words. "I own you. Like the sky owns the stars. You are mine."

He slipped the gold keyring on my finger.

"You memorize yours too?" the bishop asked, looking at me over his half moon glasses.

"Yes." I picked up the ring. "You ready, Drazen?"

"Yes."

"I, Monica Faulkner, take thee, Jonathan Drazen, to be my wedded husband, to have and to hold from this day forward, for better for worse, for richer for poorer, in sickness and in health, to love, cherish, and to obey till death. Your name is written on my heart."

I heard the murmurs. Jonathan and I had kept the word obey in my vows because we knew what we meant. He was my master in the bedroom, and I obeyed his commands. We knew the limitations between us, and these were our vows. We neither explained nor excused them.

And thus, both standing on our own two feet, before God and our families, with the news media waiting outside, we were wed.

CHAPTER 38.

JONATHAN

She was most kinetic in stasis. With her energy contained by my will and her desire to please me, she was a sizzling box of energy, and the longer I kept her there, naked and still, the closer to the skin her arousal became.

But she stayed still for me, the streets of Paris below, on the first night of our honeymoon, her nipples hard in the chilled air. I was behind her, which was all she knew. She didn't know when I'd move or what I was doing. I could hear her heart beat, and her breath, which she tried to keep even and failed. She was mine. I owned this body, this heart. I wanted to put my fingers and tongue inside her, my cock, everywhere all at once. Every act of ownership felt incomplete to the totality of my love. I married her for the second time only a day before, and I'd marry her a hundred times more, but our bond was in our consummation. I was hers and she was mine, and we only came close to the expression of the depth of it when I broke her patience, her resolve, her expectations, soothed her heart, broke her again.

I came around her, fully dressed, to watch her naked body as it shifted, to watch her eyes try to stay focused ahead. She was so good, objectifying herself for me, becoming an owned thing so we could play the games that were an expression of our deeper truth. She owned me. I was an object for her pleasure.

I sat in front of her and reached for her, brushing my fingertips across her breasts, and she shuddered. My plan was to get her on her knees and take her throat, then it all could go one of three ways, with every step leading to a new game plan, depending on her level of obedience, all leading up to the both of us quivering together. But as I ran my fingers from her breasts to her belly, something changed.

Something about her.

I kissed her navel.

She'd gained weight since starving herself in Sequoia. On our honeymoon, she was a little heavier than when we met. I knew what her body looked like and what it felt like. My hands and mouth discerned her shapes in all their perfection. And as she stood by me groaning as my tongue traced circles around her navel, I perceived a change as subtle as the sea.

"Monica," I said.

"Yes?"

"I don't want to alarm you."

She stiffened. "Are you okay?"

"*Shh.* I'm fine. As are you."

I looked up at her. She looked straight ahead, as she was supposed to, and I stood up so I could look her in the eye.

"What is it?" she asked, meeting my gaze.

"I don't want you to get excited for nothing." A senseless desire. No matter what I did, I was going to get her hopes up. I was going to risk causing disappointment and pain. I couldn't protect her from it. The greatest gift I could give Monica, a wedding gift for a life together, was hope.

She broke the silence. "Tell me or I swear I'll—"

"You'll do no such thing."

She set her mouth in a tight line and put her hands on her hips. Scene over. I took her by her

203

chin and told her what I thought, risking her dashed hopes.

"I think you're pregnant."

CHAPTER 39.

MONICA

He was impossible. From the minute he ran across Paris for a pregnancy test, to him cancelling everything on my behalf, to the doctor's appointment where I couldn't understand a word they were saying, he was the most impossible man I ever met.

"I'm fine!" I said in the square across from the doctor's office. It had a church, and a statue, and pigeons everywhere. The sky was the color of the sidewalks and the air was so wet it stuck to me. "I'm not even a little sick. I feel better than ever. I could run a marathon, so back off."

"The doctor said you should take it easy," he said. Mr. Easygoing in a blue polo, houndstooth scarf and wool coat. He was taking control of the situation, and it calmed him to be in charge, which was fine, up to a point.

"That's totally not fair. You could tell me he said I have to wear a clown suit on Tuesdays and I wouldn't even know."

"A clown suit? Even you couldn't make that sexy."

I crossed my arms and turned to face him. Pigeons flew up in a fog. The square was just starting to get crowded with the lunchtime rush, and we were ignored.

"You should have gotten me an English-speaking doctor."

"I got you the best."

"Well, I felt left out. I felt like you all were talking about me like I wasn't there. And of all people, you should understand how shitty that is."

He stepped forward and put his hands on my face, cupping my cheeks. "Do you remember that heartbeat?"

The whooshing sound, like an angel walking a heavenly treadmill had come through the sonogram loud and clear. I admitted that a tear fell from my eyes. Maybe two. Maybe I'd wept right there.

"So?" I said with a choke.

"What language was that?"

I shook my head. No language obviously. I wanted him to get to his point. "It was our baby's," he said. "It was the language of life. Who cares what the doctor and I said? Who cares how I want to take care of you? You want to fight about something? Let's fight about what you're having for lunch."

I smiled and turned my face onto his hand, kissing the palm which was warm despite the December cold.

"I want one of those ham croissants with the sour cheese," I said.

"And a salad."

"Fine."

"And after, you take one of the prenatal vitamins."

I made a yuck face. The doctor had given me bullet sized vitamins that smelled terrible. I'd take them. Jonathan was my inspiration for keeping up a regimen. I'd take them every day on a clock, but I didn't have to pretend to like it.

"I could lose it again," I whispered.

"You won't. I have a feeling this one's going to stick."

He gathered me in his arms, and we held each other in a Parisian square, rocking back and forth for blissful minutes.

CHAPTER 40.

EPILOGUE

MONICA

I woke up alone, and I panicked. I had that heavy feeling from sleeping longer and harder than I was used to. I felt drunk, hazy, and worried.

"Jonathan?" I mumbled. Was I still dreaming? Or was the air actually thicker? I knocked a glass of water from the night table. Cold water splashed on my leg. Not a dream. This was real.

How had I slept? I shouldn't have. The fact that I hadn't in three days notwithstanding, no decent person should sleep when their baby was as sick as mine was. And gone. She was gone and Jonathan, too. Had they gone to the hospital? To the ER?

Light flickered at the corner of the bedroom, under the bathroom door, and voices, no. A single voice. My husband, singing. God, he was terrible.

I opened the door.

The bathroom was washed in candlelight, and steaming hot. Jonathan was in the tub, with little Gabrielle, all of three weeks old, face up on his thighs.

"Good morning," he said. "Can you say good morning to mommy?"

Gabby snorted, then sneezed.

"How is she?"

He wielded an ear thermometer. I took it and crouched on the side of the tub. The little screen said 99.1.

"Oh," I said, "that's good. Do you think it's over?"

"I don't know." He dotted the baby's nose. "Are you finished with us, little girl?" She made an *ahhh* sound, and Jonathan turned to me. "She says yes, but she's reserving the right to change her mind."

"When did you learn to speak baby?" I ran my finger over his cheek, stripping away the water droplets.

"I live in Los Angeles."

We'd had a trying few days, with Gabby posting a 104.5 fever. Her pediatrician had come late in the night, gotten it down to 101 and gone home. We could call any time, but the ER wasn't necessary just yet. A few hours later, we were woken by the night nurse. The baby was spiking again.

It wasn't the nurse's fault, but we let her go anyway. The worry and responsibility were ours, and though we had the resources to hire out the exhaustion, we decided to own it. These were our moments of aggravation and pain. We couldn't pay someone else to being together as a family. So we stayed up all night and cared for Gabby in shifts that didn't happen, because neither of us rested. I did the night nursing, or Jonathan gave her a bottle. We were still working out a routine that my body would accept, but those moments with her were so precious, I didn't care what time of day they were.

Gabby wiggled, still not knowing what her arms were for, grabbing at air with her tiny fingers. She had a full head of black hair and though her eyes had the blue cast of a newborn's, they'd be a shade of brown.

I submerged a big yellow sponge in the warm water and squeezed it over my daughter. It fell over her chest and round belly, shining as if she'd been lacquered.

"I wanted redheaded babies," I said.

"We can try again, but unless both parents have red hair, it skips a generation."

"Why?"

"Dominance. It's in your genes."

"You're a jerk." Gabby opened her mouth and turned her head, squeaking. She was just learning to cry. She could scream, squeak, sneeze and smile, but we hadn't gotten to full blown crying without a full blown fever.

"Uh, oh," Jonathan said. "She's calling Mommy."

I peeled my shirt and underpants off. My body was still misshapen from the pregnancy, but my husband still eyeballed me as if I was the only woman in the world, and slowly, my figure was returning as if his kind attention was teasing it out.

I picked up the baby under her arms. She loved the water, and jerked her tiny legs angrily when I took her out.

"Patience, little girl," I said.

Jonathan held his arms out for me, still magnificent, wearing nothing more than a scar and an erection that was going to go unattended until the baby was fed. I got into the tub, sitting between my husband's legs. He wrapped his arms around me, and I positioned baby Gabrielle at my breast.

Jonathan rubbed my back, kissing my neck as I nursed. I was in some heavenly place, where I was cared for physically and emotionally, turning this warm tub into a slice of well being.

"Mister Gevers called," Jonathan said.

"Oh, did you thank him for the bunny and flowers?"

"Yes. He wants us to come out there. He wants to meet the little girl."

"I'm not travelling with a newborn."

"It's not that hard. I did it for ten minutes once."

"He and his wife can come here again. I'm not going anywhere yet." I leaned into him, and he wrapped his arms around us. "Not until I'm good and ready."

"Yes, mistress." He kissed my shoulder. Little Gabby nursed her little heart out. I was so in love with her, more in love than I ever thought possible. I leaned my head against my husband's chest, letting the soft warmth of the water envelope me, and somewhere in my half-sleep, I became a part of it, growing into a universe where I was loved, and where I loved. Where I was needed, and where I was allowed to need. In this tight realm of three, I dreamed myself expanding into this tiny, infinite universe, perfect in its balance and stability.

I opened my eyes when Jonathan tucked my hair behind my ear and kissed my nice. So perfect was the silence, and our baby, sated and sleeping in my arms, mouth cocked open, edges pointed in a smile.

Flesh of my flesh, love of my love, broken and tied back together with the strings of my heart, these are mine. And whatever life may bring, whatever tests and tortures, I am complete, and competent and ready to go to battle in their defense.

But for now, there is only peace.

THE END

ENDNOTES
This is an ARC – so I haven't finished these. But if you push thru there's a bonus scene at the end.

On the Drazens...I know you wanted to find out about Deirdre, Declan, Eileen, Margie, Fiona. Even Brad. And yes I know you wanted to know all about Theresa and Antonio. But I simply couldn't weave a lot of stuff in without either spoiling a future book, or painting myself into a corner. So I kept the camera tight on Jonathan and Monica. That was the only story I wanted to tell, anyway.

On the miscarriage...I am sure there are many doctors and nurses reading this. I'm also sure that there are many women who have had a variety of miscarriage experiences. Monica's is mine. Please do not nullify, belittle, or discount my experience by saying it wouldn't happen that way. Thank you.

On everyone who helped me. The list is...well, Santa would throw it back in my face. So I'm going to keep it specific to this book. TRSOR – thank you for the promotional help. I needed that off my plate. KAYLEE – shut the fuck up, girl. CANARIES – Tony and Diana thank you for maintaining my group while I sleep. ERIK – I'm so happy to have met you, and your work on my behalf is flawless. CHRISTY – Website girl – I'd recommend you everywhere but I want you all to myself (but go here if you are an author and want someone competent and talented ... http://bit.ly/1zSFj8t) LAUREN – Marketing mentor THANK YOU for your generosity. I didn't know such a big heart could fit in such a small frame. LAURELIN – Thank you for letting me steal your marketing genius for CS. FYW/BGP – I love you. CASSIE – I die without your editing. *Die.* BLOGGERS – You are my world. Thank you. I can't do anything without you guys. I'd be LOST.

BONUS SCENE

The following short was released as a Valentine's Day special for the SubClub.
The story takes place about six weeks after Jonathan's transplant. I tried to stick it in the beginning of the book, and it didn't work. Then I tried to stick it in as a memory, and that didn't work either, so here it is....

JONATHAN

I'd taken just about everything in my life for granted. Money, intelligence, women, family, but mostly, my health. I protected it easily, worked through bumps in the road and exercised when I felt like it. I ate what I wanted, when I wanted. I saw a doctor in whatever country I was travelling in, or not at all.

Mostly, not at all.

"You have a heart biopsy today." My wife mumbled, her face buried in her pillow. I brushed her hair behind her ear. I was sitting up in bed, and had been for a few hours. I didn't inherit my heart from a sleeper, apparently, and still stayed up half the night, which I was used to. What I wasn't used to was being so weak I couldn't be out of bed more than a few hours at a time.

I hated spicy food I'd loved before. I had a strange urge to run, as if the road called. I couldn't drink enough juice. All this was supposedly normal, as a rouge group of cells were peeling off the heart and sticking to my organs, but I felt way past the age when I should be discovering things about myself.

"I'm not going," I said.

"Like hell."

"I feel fine. I'm only supposed to get the biopsies if they think I'm rejecting."

She got up on her elbows. "Jonathan, let's not do this again." I could see the tops of her breasts as they fell into her white tank. We hadn't made love since I'd gotten out of the hospital. We were afraid, both of us. I didn't even know who we were sometimes.

"Let's not, then."

She rolled over onto her back. The February chill always managed to get through the old windows, the result was hard nipples pushing through her tank. She was still, as always, magnificent, and I felt a forgotten stirring.

"I'll go with you," she said, "then we can get something to eat, and you'll be back for a nap."

"You're in the studio today."

"I'll cut out. Eddie can reschedule."

My hand, as if it had a mind of its own, reached for her, brushing her nipple with the back of my fingers. It bent under them four times, then the thumb stayed, rolling it. Her eyes closed, and her mouth opened. She was the same, sensitive as a raw nerve ending, but she wouldn't let me touch her until recently. I'd satisfied her twice since then, but we couldn't do more together because of the nagging, overwhelming fear.

"You are not to reschedule again or ever," I said, pinching the nipple.

"You have to go for the biopsy." She groaned it. I was hard. Very hard.

"No, I don't." I yanked at her panties. "Take these off."

She looked at me for a second, brown eyes big as coffee cups. She grabbed at the sides of her underwear and wiggled out of them. She'd started gaining her weight back, and though the sickly gauntness was gone, her hip bones still jutted too far under her skin, and the space between her thighs was too apparent. Getting something to eat probably wasn't a bad idea, except I wasn't getting another fucking biopsy.

She was still on her back, all hard nipples and hidden cunt. I didn't know if I could. I mean, physically, I was cleared for fucking, but I still didn't feel right. "Legs spread, knees up. Come on. Let me see."

She did as she was told, as always, and I slid my hand down her belly, past her triangle, to her waiting lips. She gasped.

"You're fucking soaked. I never met a woman who needed to fuck so bad."

"Get the biopsy. God, please." Her head was thrown back. "I'll suck your cock right now."

"You're not using sex to bribe me are you?"

"I am, I am."

Good, great God she needed a spanking. I knew six months ago I would have welted her for doing what she was doing, but I didn't think I could take any kind of intensity. I knew my heart wouldn't pound since the vagus nerve was cut, but having her clit under my fingers without feeling a racing heart as accompaniment to my desire was disconcerting. I felt dead at the same time as I felt on the precipice of life.

I took my fingers from her and placed them on her lips, glossing them with her juice. She opened her mouth and sucked on them. I was about to spontaneously combust, but I couldn't. Not yet. I was still not myself, still afraid, like a child. I was ashamed of my fear, but not ashamed enough to conquer it.

I put my hand between her legs again, sliding inside her, up to her clit and back. Her hand stroked between my thighs.

I squeezed her clit, and she arched her back, then I touched the tip of it.

"Let me suck you," she gasped. "Please. I'll go slow."

"No."

I flattened my fingers against her, pushed two into her cunt, moving her clit with my palm, then out again, and back.

"Look at me," I said. She opened her eyes, and I leaned down to kiss her. Her mouth tasted like cunt and her tongue tasted like morning. "Say my name."

"Jonathan."

I put three fingers in her, and drew them out. She squeaked.

"Jonathan."

"Come."

I moved faster, harder.

"Jonathan. Oh. Jonathan."

She arched her back, pushing her arms over her, crying out my name. Music, but with half an orchestra.

***

The technician breezed in wearing scrubs and a full suit of medical detachment. She was young and attractive, with no makeup and straight brown hair pulled back in an efficient ponytail. I had the best team in the world, and they treated me like just any other patient. I guess that was what I was paying them for.

"We're going in through the arm today," she said through her mask.

"That's what the doctor said."

"Are we doing the gas?"

Jesus fucking Christ, save me from the habitual pluralization of experience.

"Nope."

"It's going to be uncomfortable." Her tag said Fran. A bland name. It suited her.

"We'll manage." God, I was cranky.

Fran got her tray of sharp things in front of her and I laid my arm out. My first biopsy had been through the jugular vein. I suspected this would feel less invasive. More like a walk in the park while a tube snaked through my body.

The swab was cold on my skin, and I went into meat mode, where I went someplace else in my mind while I was treated like a side of beef.

"So," she said, beginning the small talk that preceded painful invasions. "We're married, I see." She pointed to my ring. "What are we doing for Valentine's Day?"

I didn't answer.

"Mister Drazen? Are you okay?"

I think the word "you" as opposed to "we" woke me faster than the real concern in her voice.

"It's the fourteenth?"

"Yup," she said, dicking with her plastic and metal tinkertoys.

"Shit."

"We're going to the Getty Center. They have this romantic dinner prix fix on the patio. They put candles on the fountain and they have a really nice string quartet."

"Shit," I repeated. "I forgot."

"Oh. Well. Maybe we can still get it together in time? Going in now, we'll just feel a little pinch."

She got the stent in with barely a nip. Pluralization or no, she was good. She snapped the gloves off. "All done. Doctors will be back in a minute. Do you want the info for the Getty? I don't think there will be space, but maybe someone cancelled?"

"Thanks, Fran. I'm good."

***

Doctor Solis knew better than to kill me with "we" and "our" or small talk. He wanted me in and out of there as much as I wanted to go, and the two other doctors in the room seemed equally sensitive to Solis's dominance in that room.

"Any changes?" he asked, eyes on the monitor, fingers on keys as Doctor Nu slipped the thin tube through the stent. "Still off spicy food?"

"Hate it."

"Too bad. How's the wind been on your allergies?"

"I don't have allergies." I felt the tube in me, slipping across my shoulder through a vein. It was truly uncomfortable. Not painful, but I had to think hard to not try and claw through my skin to get the invading thing out.

"Chart says different." He checked Dr. Nu's work and looked at me. "You need to pay attention. Denial is your enemy. Your silly new allergies can turn into an infection you won't be able to fight. With the drought, and the wind, my wife is eating Claritin like candy, even in the middle of February."

"Valentine's Day," I said more to myself than him.

"Any plans?" Dr. Solis asked, one hand on the tube, eyes on the tube, then the screen, then back.

"We're in," Dr. Nu called, and I felt it.

"Indeed," Solis said. "Breathe, Mister Drazen. Breathe."

***

How fast could I pull something together? Something huge. Something the size of my love, my respect, my devotion. It was our first Valentine's together, and Christmas had been such a disaster, that I felt as if I needed to make it up to Monica tenfold. But when I got home from the biopsy, Lil had to help me to the door.

"Where's the Missus today?" she asked. "Do you need me to get her?"

"Leave her alone. She's in the studio." She put me on the couch, and my body wanted to stay there forever.

"Mister Drazen, I don't want to pressure you, but I hope you didn't forget—"

"I forgot."

"I can pick up a dozen roses."

"Sure, Lil. Sure. Great idea."

She left to do the impossible, find a dozen roses on Valentine's Day for a man so enervated he couldn't do it himself.

"Fuck you," I whispered to heaven, my first sentiment of ingratitude in two months. "I'm getting over this."

My recovery was on track. I had no reason to be so angry, except that I was cheating Monica out of her entitlements, and her number one entitlement was me. From that couch to the stars above, I owed her myself.

I picked up the phone and called my friend Paul. We spoke briefly, and then I closed my eyes for a few hours.

***

I woke with a buildup behind my face, and a sneeze.

They say your heart skips a beat when you sneeze, so when I sneezed four more times, I panicked unreasonably. Then I panicked again when I realized the sun was setting and I was still on the couch.

"Fuck!"

Next to me, a dozen red roses, beautifully arranged, and an empty card and a pen on the table. Thank God for Lil. I needed to give her more money.

I picked up my phone. Sneezed again. Multiple texts from Monica.

—*Still here*—

—*Will be late*—

—*How did the biopsy go?*—

—*Great session. Do you want dinner with me for Valentine's? Or are we skipping?*—

—*Where are you?*—

219

*—Please just tell me
you're ok or I'm leaving
the studio right now—*

The last one had been minutes before and had
probably gotten me to wake up. I tapped a fast
response so she wouldn't panic. She panicked when
I didn't respond, or when I breathed too hard, or
slept too much or too little.

—Just got up—

*—thank you thank you
thank you—*

*—Let me stretch and we'll talk
about tonight—*

*—No pressure but I hope
it involves your cock in my
mouth—*

*—But if not then ok I
love you—*

I sneezed when I smiled. It was the fucking
roses. Snot built up behind my face. My sinuses felt
like they were going to explode. According to my
doctors, if the buildup settled in my sinuses or
lungs, my suppressed immune system would allow

an infection. And like everything else in the goddamn universe, it could kill me. So I threw the roses out.

***

I'd sent Lil to pick up Monica an hour before. It was Friday, so traffic from the west side would be brutal. From my vantage point at the Griffith Park Observatory, I could see the city in all its jam-packed glory. Streetlights held their grid, and the car lights along Wilshire crawled. She was there, somewhere, on her way to me.

I hoped I'd pulled this off as if I'd planned better. Paul, the director of the Observatory, had taken me to a stone veranda inaccessible to the public, letting caterers in to set up a dinner for two overlooking Los Angeles. I had candles, heat lamps, chafing dishes, everything I could manage for her. Below me, clusters of tourists shifted on well-worn paths, their laughter and voices drifting up to me without meaning. They'd be gone in an hour when the museum closed and we'd be here, on our perch above the city.

I'd texted and called, letting her know Lil would pick her up, but I hadn't heard back. Once I told her I was fine, she probably shut the phone off to work. I considered the possibility that she was still in the studio, and would be until the wee hours of the morning, in which case I'd pack up dinner and go home, grateful she'd forgotten the holiday as well.

My phone rang.

"Hi, Lil. Where are you?"

"She's gone, sir. Sorry, I've been looking, but it turns out she left."

"Thanks. Head home. She probably went there."

I called my wife, confident I wasn't disturbing studio time.

"Goddess?"

"Where are you?"

"I'm at a surprise location. Lil is—"

"You have to come home," she said, her voice raspy from a day abusing it.

"No, you have to come here."

"Jonathan."

"Monica."

"I spent a week on this."

I argued a little more after that, but she'd spent time on whatever it was, whereas I'd thrown something together because a medical technician reminded me of the date eight hours before. I had the staff pack everything up.

***

Lil had gotten to me quickly. She pulled up to the front, but didn't go past the gate.

"Can you make it in from here?" she called back. "I'm not supposed to go past the gate."

"You knew?"

"Well, no. I just got a call. She thought you'd be napping this time, but then this whole thing happened instead. Sorry. At least you have the roses I picked up."

"Thank you, by the way."

"My pleasure."

I got out. The gate had a door-sized entry and I went in that way. All the front lights were out, but Monica had put little paper lights along the drive, and I followed them to the house.

"They were going to go down the stairs," she said. "But they're fine outside too."

She was naked, on my porch.

Our porch.

"I love what you're wearing," I said.

"My mom got it for me." She put her hands behind her back. Did I think she was too thin? She was perfect, her skin lit by candles and the moon, her hair falling over her shoulders like a scarf.

I got on the step below and touched her belly.

"You poor woman," I said, kissing the space between her breasts. Peaches and honey. Her scent. I rubbed her skin, releasing it, putting my tongue on her nipple and sucking. My hands went down her back, until I reached her clasped fingers. I took hers in mine.

"I need you, Jonathan. I had a whole speech prepared. But I forgot it."

"I'm sorry you had to wait."

"Can you take me? Please."

"No pressure?"

She reached for my crotch, and I let her.

"Oh, you're hard."

"Very."

She pulled me to a chair and sat me down. She got on her knees. Nothing could have pleased me more than her, naked, on my porch, kneeling before me. I put my hands in her hair as she took my dick out. I didn't like her controlling the situation, but maybe it was the new heart that didn't find it that offensive. Maybe I'd changed in more ways than one.

Her mouth was eager, her throat, open for an aria. Her hands stayed behind her back. I knew what I would have done before the surgery. I would have jammed her head onto me. I would have gone fast, just because it made it more difficult for her to manage. I would have been hard and cruel and derived satisfaction from her discomfort. But not that day.

She looked up at me, letting my dick pop out of her mouth.

"Is it ok?"

"Get up here," I said. "Straddle me. Let's give this a go."

"Really?"

"Don't make me say it twice."

She was up in a flash, thighs around me, eager hands around my base.

"Fuck, Jonathan. You're so hard."

I put my hands on either side of her face and brought it to mine. "I own you," I whispered.

"I love you, too." She hitched herself up, until the head of my dick was at her opening and her hands were on the back of the chair. "Are you ready?"

"Yes." I put downward pressure on my hands, and gingerly and slowly, she lowered herself onto me. She was wet and tight, and when she pulled out, the sensation of being pleasurably sucked overwhelmed me. I groaned. She slid down, then up again. We kissed, then breathed on each other's faces, kissed again.

I put my thumb on her clit, stroking up and down as she moved against me. In my life, I came when I wanted to, and not a minute before. I listened for any number of physical signs so I knew when to hold back. One of them was my heart rate. So when the buildup in my groin happened without a feeling in my chest, I missed the opportunity to catch myself.

"I'm sorry," I moaned. "I'm coming."

"Come for me."

She moved faster. I wasn't in control. My body was betraying me. I had to give it up, again.

I came so hard I called her name to heaven.

Then, I sneezed.

"Bless you."

"Tha—"

Sneeze.

"Bless—"

Sneeze.

"How many more you got?"

I shrugged behind my hand. *Sneeze.*

She got off me. "Let me get you a tissue." She was up and through the front door before I could tell her I had a hankie and then I knew what caused the sneezing. I got up and stood in the doorway.

The living room was bedecked in roses.

She trotted down the stairs, still naked, carrying a box of tissues. "You were supposed to see this first. But I wasn't about to say no on the porch."

Sneeze.

She handed me the box.

"Monica, I'm—" *Sneeze.* I waved my hand at a cluster of yellow roses. "Why the yellow?"

"There's a red rose for every day I've known you. A yellow for every day you were in the hospital. And one white." She swallowed hard and her mouth screwed up to one side. "For the day I thought you died." Her eyes went wet.

I successfully held back a sneeze.

"I know what you think," she said. "I know you're worried about the recovery. And our sex life. You think you're hiding it and being all strong, but I can see it. I wanted to let you know, well, before I seduced you, that it didn't matter. It takes what it takes. I'll wait forever for you. Every day, I'm glad you're alive."

"My goddess. I'm so sorry." I kissed her before she could protest, then sneezed again. "We have to get rid of the roses, but first, I'm taking you upstairs. I'm fucking you as much as you deserve."

"You're dressed up." She stepped back and looked me up and down. It was as if she saw me for the first time. "Where were you when you called?"

"Not telling. It's the idea for your birthday dinner now."

"I ruined your Valentine's dinner."

"I'm throwing your roses out."

"We suck at this."

I sneezed, and took her upstairs to fuck her as much as she deserved. And she deserved a lot.

To check out the rest of the series, see my
Amazon author page

Part 2 is due out in early March, 2013.

To keep up with what I think is sexy today, see
my facebook page

www.facebook.com/CDReiss.writer

Email me at cdreiss.writer@gmail.com

If you'd like to be notified of new releases,
which are run at a discount during launch week,
send me your email address.

And, of course, if you have any feelings about
this book you'd like to share, kindly leave a review.

39513643R00139

Made in the USA
Charleston, SC
09 March 2015